The Essence of Longing

Book 2 of To Hold a Flower

Written by Caroline Sophia Hamel

Copyright © 2023 Caroline Hamel

To request permissions, contact the publisher at caroline@carolinesophiahamel.com

ISBN (Paperback Edition): 9798986273914
ISBN (eBook Edition): 9798986273921
Library of Congress Control Number: 2022921956

Cover Art by © mihaellustrates
Edited by © I.O. Scheffer

First printing edition 2023

Place of Publication: Bellingham, Washington

For Luke Shealy,

You're an amazingly thoughtful, kind, and considerate person that I feel comfortable and supported around and I'm so grateful to have in my life. It's hard to think of a better person to be friends with. You inspire me, you've been there for me, and you've given me a lasting friendship that I'm grateful to share.

A Brief Guide to Pronunciation

ie – Used in a name, pronounced as a hard E and then a soft e (Liela is Lee-ell-uh)

y – Used in a name, pronounced as a soft i (Myllia is Mill-ee-uh)

u – Used in a name, pronounced as a hard U (Dunet is Dune-et or Dew-net)

ei – Used in a name, pronounced as you would pronounce air, heir, or their (example – Veir)

Content Warnings / Trigger Warnings

Suicidal Ideation, Implied Self-Harm, Self-Harm Imagery, Depression, Anxiety, self-hate, self-loathing, Ableism, Internalized Ableism

Please Skip to Avoid Major Spoilers

****

Trigger Warning for parents disowning their queer child.

****

~

While my intention is for my characters to find self-love, some readers may find the content in this & the following parts upsetting, too heavy, or too personal to engage with.

~

Be advised that The Essence of Longing & the following releases of To Hold a Flower will heavily deal with suicide in a very personal & extensive way. My intention is to deal with this topic as sensitively as I can. It's something personal to me & it's very important to me that I deal with it well.

~

I do not fault you if you are not ready to engage with this material. To those of you who do & those who don't:

I hope that you can find healing & a way to love yourself.

& in Addition to that Content Warning, a Content Advisory:

Content Advisory

This book contains sexual content and two sex scenes. If you are not ready for these, they are found in two chapters: "In a Gentle World" and "Time That Stops," plus there is another chapter heavily bordering into a sex scene, but without it actually taking place ("Pain Grasping at a Heartbeat") and "Time That is Ours" has heavy sexual meaning. While these provide important emotional beats and intimate moments for the characters, they are not a necessary read, but they are important to both characters' arcs and the thematic / messaging elements of this book. The actual sex is only about 4 pages worth of content. The majority of the two chapters with sex are internal monologue. In the end, the maturity level you are ready for and what you want to read is up to reader digression.

We lose ourselves

And find ourselves

In a tumbling tide

It ebbs and flows

Longing for sunbeams

Or falling into dark depths

Alone

Or embraced

Slowly falling apart

Piecing ourselves together

Or just holding on

Who we are

And who we want to be

Those choices spiral

As we drown

Fight our way

Or stand surely

Lost

Or found

In reaching hands

To draw close

Or drift apart

It hurts

Its exhilarating

Numbing

Hopeful

But through this tunnel

The you that you will be is somewhere out there

The you beyond this day

And beyond your tumbling heart

To move through it all

Is something you must do

Caroline Sophia Hamel

I should have apologized to Liela ...

And now I hate myself for it.

I really am ... such a selfish person.

Caroline Sophia Hamel

Caroline Sophia Hamel

Caroline Sophia Hamel

The Darkness We Welcome

Dunet

My hands curl over the wall, barely registering the frigid cold of the stone. I watch Liela and Myllia in the dancing lights of fireflies through the dark night. A glow surrounds them in the grass, as they sit close, cradled amid the stalks rustling in the breeze.

I stand there rigidly, feeling so far away. I look upon their warmth that I want to feel.

This cradled darkness softly kisses me.

I want to bury myself far away.

Why do my eyes sting so harshly when I look at them?

What is there to hate in their love?

There is only me to hate.

I want to crush myself.

Did I mean anything I said about what and who I would be? Or what I would do?

A knife threads my thoughts. I had thought that I meant it ... but now I think I really hadn't.

I should have apologized to Liela.

I am a terrible person for not doing that. But something holds me back from doing it ...

And even though I shouldn't, I let it.

Maybe there's a part of myself that just wants to feel numb?

I turn away from Liela and Myllia, and I sink against the wall, pulling my knees into a hug as I stare forward vacantly.

I hope for something to happen, but I'm not even sure what. Whatever it might be, it won't come.

I hear the muffled sound of boots, then turn my head up.

Kind, deep blue eyes search my face. His pleasant, broad grin stirs up a smile on my lips, although I first refuse to let it show. "It's been a while, Dunet."

"Who are you?" I croak, parsing a smile to my lips, as I know it's rude not to smile for someone. I don't recognize him for a moment. My brain is fuzzy.

"*Lord* Darnor Veln," he proclaims smoothly, running a hand through his elegant brown hair. "And don't tell Liela I used it that way."

The curtain falls back from my eyes a little more, and my smile fractures. "I remember you," I say in a small voice. "Sorry."

"I don't mind at all." He moves to sit down next to me. "You know that Liela talks about you more than anyone."

I nod as if through syrup.

"And you know, I'm nothing next to her. Her and Driena tease me constantly, but I know that they're there for me beneath their cruelty." There's a sweet fondness to his words. "We always have and will be friends and I know Liela might go far sometimes ... But I'll be okay with that, because I know it doesn't mean anything. Do you get what I'm trying to say?"

My chest rises unsteadily, and I nod. "Maybe? I think I do. But ..."

"Dunet, your sister thinks you're ready. She hates leaving you and she talked for years of putting it off. I think Driena was too harsh on her for it ... and I let it go. I think that's best for both of you." He smiles magnificently. "Dunet ... I know Liela is a lost cause sometimes, but she always means well."

"It's not that ..."

"Oh?" He turns his head to me thoughtfully.

The stars seem so pale behind him.

I sink my head deeper into my knees. "I don't think you should hear that. I want you to forget." Hopefully, he won't ask me any more questions. I scrunch my eyes, hoping he'll go away.

"I doubt you want me or anyone to see you like this. But Dunet"—I hear his whisper softening as he gives me a light pat on my head— "it's okay to not be perfect. Remember that."

17

My heart locks up as I shrink away from him, wanting so much to hide from his words. I wish he hadn't seen me. No one should see this darkness of mine. I hear the brush of fabric and the sliding of his limbs off the wall, then his hand leaves my head.

I pry my head from my knees and turn to catch his back with my watering eyes. I see him as if through a far tunnel. My eyes shimmer dangerously, and he falls away into shadow.

For a flicker of an instant, he had kindled something small and vulnerable in my heart.

I close my eyes and crush it.

A Dance to Heal Your Heart

Myllia

I stroke her hair as she looks at the dazzling flickers through the grasses, like tiny green lanterns through a miniscule forest.

We lay in the cool night air, the crumpled, golden stalks of grass brushing against our entwined fingers.

Her eyes are soft and distant and so tenderly lost. "Myllia …" she whispers like a prayer, turning her beautiful olive eyes up to me.

"Liela …" I whisper back. I know that all she needs is a confirmation that I'm here.

She closes her eyes and breathes in deeply. "I feel so lost, Myllia … But you make me feel weightless. I just want tomorrow to come … Oh, I know that won't change anything. I don't know this person she showed me, Myllia. It scares me."

"I know it does." I cradle her head, drawing us closer in the soft patch of lantern light, under the pale moon and swirling stars. "But now you know another part of her, and all you can do is embrace it …"

"That is what I'm scared of. Maybe I pushed her away …?" Her voice sounds broken for a moment. She looks up at the night sky, frowning in distress.

I nestle closer to her ear. "Liela, you did not push her away. You never could have done that. Whatever she needs, she needs you."

"Myllia ..." Her head grazes my shoulder when she turns to face me again. "I want to feel like we did that night. I want to hold you again. I know it's nothing but avoiding what I need to do, but I think I need this."

My heart beats lightly in my chest. She looks a little blurry in my eyes, set tenderly against the light of the fireflies.

Sitting up, I draw away from her gently. I feel her hands rest on my shoulders when she sits up too, and her breath meets mine. My breath catches. She looks at me with eyes that are so unfocused. I bring my forehead against hers and giggle softly, as if that will let her know that everything is okay.

She brings her hand up to my cheek and I lean into it.

"Liela ..." I whisper her name and she smiles. I pull her in as we sit up in the grass, under the light of the moon, fireflies weaving a magical tapestry around us. I press my hand against her cheek, too, before loosely wrapping my arms around her neck. My heart picks up with the breeze.

We draw apart and I slide my hands into hers, rising into an embrace while on our feet. I take a step away, then I twirl around, looking playfully at her. I return to holding her hands, and we rock gently through the sweeping grasses as they ripple in beads of a thousand tiny lights.

My breath is so light; I feel kissed by the stars. I want her tender warmth forever.

Liela slows down and looks at me—it's magical how beautiful her eyes look, even in their turmoil.

"Is there anything else I can do, Liela?"

Her mouth pulls up at the corners. "This is all you need to do, Myllia. You help me when I'm lost."

Her eyes seep into my heart, making it feel just as bright and delicate as the moon through a still night.

"Myllia ... you know I love you so much."

Her words make my heart flutter. "I love you too, Liela. You are the most beautiful, kindhearted person I know."

She leans into my shoulder, and I let out a deep breath. She seems so fragile here in the cold, piecing herself back together bit by bit.

"Myllia, let's go inside. I'm exhausted."

I know her exhaustion comes from much more than the cold.

She pulls away, then we drop our hands into each other's and entwine them.

We walk by the torches and lanterns of the castle wall, then the stables come back into view.

It seems much darker here than in that sea of light.

Liela stiffens. She draws her hand away, before breathing in and tucking it back in mine, sending a chill down my spine.

I squeeze her hand once more. "It will all be all right, Liela."

Silent, she nods and we make our way up the wide steps of the castle, past the dome entryway glowing with dim lantern flames, then up the winding steps to Liela's warmly lit suite.

Liela slows near her room, as if reluctant to leave me. I'm excited at the thought of being so close to where Liela sleeps.

She pauses, then turns to face me at the door.

My smile blooms and I rise on my toes to kiss her cheek.

"Myllia." She pulls me in, as my chest squeezes in a fuzzy feeling. "Thank you."

"Liela, I just want you to know that you are a beautiful person."

She looks up with glistening eyes. "I'll miss you tonight, Myllia."

My heart sinks into her words. "I will miss you too, Liela." I giggle, tracing her with my lashes.

She turns away from me, and her eyes stay with me for as long as they can.

"I love you, Liela," I whisper, as she closes her bedroom door behind her.

It is only then that the weight of the day catches up with me.

Liela

I look at my bed, hesitant.

I needed Myllia today. She ... I couldn't have gotten through today without her.

I just don't know what to do.

My hand clenches, then slackens. I collapse onto my bed, not caring what I'm wearing. I just want to sleep, and I let my eyes droop, for I'm stumbling. I don't know what to do anymore ...

I'm afraid to fall.

A Warm Hand

Liela

I sit at my desk, shuffling through paperwork in the late hours of the night.

For once, I just want to rest … to slow down and be at peace. But I also want the day to whirl by and pick me up with it, so I don't have to think about the hurt on Dunet's face every time I close my eyes.

I take a shaky breath and cast my eyes down at my quill. I grip it in a vise.

I breathe in and let my hand relax, then stare past the window at the stars cradling the Kalltarris Mountains … Stars that are far too silent and steady, when I feel far from that same restful peace that I had thought I'd found.

I pull my eyes back down, and my chair creaks forward. I rest my hand over my brow and scan another document from the ever-growing pile of paperwork.

It's a letter from one of the scouts. I search every line, and my chest sinks with it. Nothing … Silence. It's unsettling, but not unexpected and changes nothing.

I need news. I need something.

My eyes settle on the map again—it's resting on the edge of the desk. My left hand brushes within a breadth of it, but only trails there.

There's been no response yet from Siltheus, the capital city of Mathar. As far as I know, we're alone. Yes, I know this was planned.

Our correspondence must have been intercepted. I grit my teeth, tilting my head back. There's nothing I can do. I let out a heavy sigh.

I could send a larger force. Maybe I will, but not yet, not when so much could go wrong, and I need as many soldiers stationed here as possible. We are on the front lines, and we need all the defense we have ... I can't defend anyone by stretching myself thin. It feels like a waiting game, all the pieces so elusive, but so ominous. No matter how fortified we are, I still worry that this could be something even we cannot withstand without aide.

I give another brief sigh. My mind is so preoccupied lately that there is almost no room left in its crowded confines. I have so much to think about and my body just screams at me to rest, for even a passing moment ... to just close my eyes. I can barely keep track of it all.

On top of all of it, I have Dunet. I really want to think of her more, but my duties keep me from her—I'm pent up in meetings and with paperwork. I want to think we have healed the rift between us, but I still find it agonizing to think about.

I feel the brush of air. I'm so tired that I must have missed the door.

Myllia ... Her presence calms my mind.

She lingers, but doesn't interrupt. Her presence is welcome. I feel all the weight lift from my shoulders, if only for a moment …

I lean back. The hours finally set in; the candle on my desk burns low.

"You should get some sleep." Her smile reminds me of our courtyard memories of spring and summer.

I turn to her, not allowing my own exhaustion to deny her my own smile.

She lays a hand on my shoulder and pulls my thoughts far away from my desk. Her eyes dance over me. "Even a commander needs her rest. You need your strength, Liela."

I soak in the warmth of her hand, my eyelids too heavy to keep open for more than a few seconds at a time. I admit that, even for me, this is enough … I won't be doing anyone any good like this. "What are you doing up this late, Myllia?"

"I wanted to give you some company. I had a feeling you would still be up, working your hardest."

My heart swells; at times, she is so thoughtful that my chest could burst. I give in, folding the letters and sorting the paperwork into cabinets. Then I stand, resting my fingers under the rim of the candle as I lift it off the desk, shadows wavering playfully against the walls and illuminating her generous curves.

Myllia smiles sweetly at me, the curls by her ears tenderly illuminated in the light. Her cornflower eyes are delicate in a way that takes my breath away.

I blow out the candle and she leans forward. "Liela ..." Her giggle is a bell in the darkness.

I touch her hands, then fold them in mine.

She comes in for a kiss, and my lips tingle as I kiss her back. She pulls away and I let go, a sigh held on my lips. "No ... I know I should sleep, Myllia."

"Good night, Liela." I can hear her drift out of the room, taking the peaceful sensation of her heartbeat with her, leaving me alone to find sleep.

My eyes linger on her retreating back. I wish she would stay ...

But my words catch too far back in my throat to ask ... My heart is pounding unbelievably loud.

It aches every time she leaves. My only solace is that I think she feels the same way.

A Struggling Smile

Dunet

Everything looks so harsh and so plain, always muted and gray, even when the sun shines, my world is paling.

But I push through it. I don't know why everyone else still sees my eyes shining brightly, my step light, and my cheeks rosy. It was always an act … It had to be.

Because it is so draining to hold every little piece together. I have to. There is hardly a reason why. It doesn't stir my soul when I bring a smile to someone's face. It rings hollowly, like a far-off bell resounding in my chest, keeping me prancing my way forward on heavy feet, just enough to find another small reason to go on.

My world is an illusion. It is an illusion that I want my sister to weave for me. I want her to sing it for me, so that I know I have a place where I'm needed and where things make sense.

I would let my shoulders droop, let my smile fade and my eyes crack, if I were alone …

But that wouldn't do, so I force my steps away from my room whenever I can. I go anywhere. To Eriena, the kitchens, the fields, the courtyards, my classes, Halfern …

Although, I've even been avoiding Myllia. I love her … I really do, but I don't want to ruin what she has with my sister. If anything, it holds my mind together to see them cradled in each other's love. They're so far from my numb fingers that are barely grasping still ... They're happier than I could ever be.

So happy that they forget about me in their fairytale. They can still feel the warmth of the sun.

The sun's touches are fading from my skin, as I embrace all the shadows that I'm discovering around me.

I'm avoiding Liela too.

Not enough to break her beautiful illusion that I wish was real, but enough so that my smile slowly fades back in ... Or, at least, I hope my smile shows. I know that if I hold it long enough, she will see what she wants, not because she wants to hurt me, but because she thinks I heal much easier than I do.

I should have been able to pull myself out of my thoughts by now.

Nothing is wrong. No, I suppose there is one thing wrong ... Myself.

I sink my eyes into the cage of my fingers to block out the world.

I wouldn't have caused Liela this pain if I weren't here.

Sometimes I just wish I could disappear, as if there was never any of me that existed ... Nothing for anyone to remember me by.

Everything would be perfect.

I'm the gap in their happiness.

I try to create something, only to pull it away.

What they see is a distortion.

Maybe I just wanted to fill myself with their smiles …

Yet, it never worked.

The me that's here can't reach their smiles … How can I be someone other than myself, at my core? I don't understand what I'm supposed to do with the people around me, who see whatever they want to see. My relationships are imaginary, like the "me" they know.

Everything passes through me, and I have nothing to give. I let my fingers slip from my face and stare blankly ahead.

I'm just an empty smile with empty, meaningless words, painting them dully from a stiff mind, where everything beyond simple desires passes through me and vanishes. For an unexplainable reason, I'm unable to comprehend any more than that. All else is lost in blurry objects that I want to know but can't process.

I'm nothing and I deserve nothing.

Right now, I just want Myllia to whisk Liela away, into clouds that blur her memories of me, until she is standing above me with all her dreams intact and untainted, the fairytale she held of me forgotten.

If only it were so simple not to be here.

I will hold my smile for as long as I can, while inside I am blindly falling into shadow, and all the world's light pales in my eyes.

This *dullness* keeps *scraping* at my eyes.

Sometimes I get the urge to stab them or put as much pressure against them as I can, so as not to feel anything but that ... to see nothing but this familiar darkness.

But I know what everyone would think if I did.

They would think me insane ... that I needed help.

And I don't want that.

I don't need that.

All I can do is hold my eyes open.

Even if it burns, it's better than the silence behind them.

Numbly, I gaze around the classroom, and I have to shake myself every so often to remain present.

I furtively tuck my head and dart my eyes. Sylvia sits to my left, and she hasn't seemed to notice me. Her cheek rests lazily on her splayed palm, head cocked with fluttering, dreamy eyes, and single braid trailing on the desk. I sigh, then quickly shut my mouth. The sunlight seems to trail just as lazily over her.

I turn, then duck my eyes as I register the gaze of the person next to me. I look up again and stitch a smile to my face. Lily stares at me, seawater eyes too clear on me under her straightened bangs. Her gaze makes me want to squirm. She still dresses in a brown dress, with her auburn, braided pigtails, sunhat, and basket. I have always liked her look. I want to be friends with her, but something about her … unnerves me. She makes me feel cold, despite her warm appearance.

She opens her mouth as if to say something, only to snap it shut, then turn away.

A moment later, I realize I have been holding my breath, and I let one out.

Lily points one foot down, toes at the floor, while the other swings freely like a pendulum.

She darts one more glance at me, and I look away.

When I turn back, she's looking out the window, head tilted back in a way that mystifies me.

I hate it when she notices me.

No, not her, I suppose … but whatever she noticed.

What did I do wrong? What do I need to fix?

How can I hide the fact that I'm not here? That I'm far away, only distantly registering the people around me.

My breath catches before picking up sharply. I bring my eyes up, gripping my wrist under the desk to quiet myself.

Sometimes I wish I were invisible.

All I have is what I can draw out of others.

Maybe that's an awful thing to wish? Maybe I'm just taking.

But the more I can act, the more real their reactions and my performances feel. At least, I would like for everything happening on the outside to feel as real as the emptiness inside me.

My smile can never slip, but I wish it didn't bite at my skin.

The Timidity of Affection

Torie

It's been a little while since my exam. I'm glad I passed, but I can't help thinking of my choice to send Dunet and Kreenie away.

Maybe it was irresponsible of me? Or at least I should've known better. Though, I always think I'm doing what's best for them both, but Dunet takes it too hard, and Kreenie ... Well, she's Kreenie.

I smile when I picture Kreenie, *my chest warming up as if she was giving me the biggest hug in the world*. She wouldn't know the difference, if I was hurting her or being kind. In some ways, that's a relief; I don't have to dwell too much on my actions toward her. Then again, if she was to hurt because of me, I don't know what I would do to make it up to her.

My shoulders sag and I sigh. I push up my glasses. No use thinking about it. I did what I thought was right.

Still, Kreenie is my best friend. I *could* start being more fair to her. I really want to try.

Whatever I do, I just know that I can't give up on her. She needs my help ... She always has.

That's just her. She's different, and she always will be. I'm only now starting to accept this, but I think I've always known deep down.

And ... maybe I missed her a little during my exam, but her and Dunet are very similar.

What am I doing? I thought I'd push them together? Where was the harm in that?

Nevertheless, I worry about them both, especially Dunet. Kreenie's odd, but she's always been confident in who she is. Dunet reminds me of myself up until a few years ago.

I pick at the frames of my glasses. It hits a bit too close to home, but Dunet tells me she hasn't been bullied.

I don't believe her.

No ... I could never believe that. But what could I say or do once that line of conversation was cut short?

At least she has good people looking after her. I smile. Darnor. He said he was her friend. It threw me off a little when he told me her only friend was Liela—something I had started to pick up on, but it shouldn't have been the case.

Because of Darnor, I had Kreenie talk to Dunet about getting friends. I do know that was irresponsible, but I can't bring myself to tell her myself ... my words just won't come.

I sigh again, turning back to my work and trying to dismiss my thoughts. I know they'll nag at me. I can't help feeling a kinship with Dunet. What if something goes wrong for her and she needs my help?

Regardless, I do wish a little bit that they were there with me when I passed. I celebrated with Kreenie and Lunan afterwards.

I look up. Chef Feln bustles through the throng of the kitchen with a smile on his face, steam wafting around the room.

I look across the room at Kreenie. I feel a protective urge to get close to her again. It's harder for her to get in trouble while I'm around, but at least most of the kitchen staff accommodates her. Kreenie is all the way across the room—bubbly, talkative, and flamboyant.

I still worry about being so far away. Kreenie is clueless sometimes, but Chef Feln gave me permission to train with her. Most of the time I'm able to be with her, but now that I've graduated, I can't always be and it's frustrating sometimes.

Right now I'm with the older cooks. I look to my left at Marta as she smiles at me.

It's a new feeling. I smile to myself. But I'm very glad I graduated. I'm getting along well with my career. Overall it's a good change.

Star-Souls

Liela

My forehead creases as I look at my paperwork, and sigh. The gray light of midday shines dimly through the office onto the proud, but rickety, wood. This office seems as aged as I sometimes feel working in it—it hosts a respectable, calming presence that reminds me of Commander Wheln.

I shake my head, chiding myself again. He is no longer my superior.

It is a small and muffled office, but I like that. It's not too small to feel cramped. Formal and old-fashioned, but a little shabby. I kept some of Wheln's sense of space intact to remind me of him and all his lessons.

I still have some trinkets of my own, though not much. I left Dunet's preserved flower crown from late summer in my own room, but here I have a portrait of when we were younger. Father gave it to me not too long ago and I can't help yearning at how young and childlike Dunet still looks in it. I saved every card from her, just like mother and father. Dunet's letters are all so sweet and maybe a little bit scatter-brained—a bit whimsical, but kind and loving and full of light and warmth in every word. I know it was true to an extent.

And, from my grandmother—a locket I always keep near me, but never wear. I also keep her favorite storybook—a whimsical one with a bunny and a girl that I used to read to Dunet. Grandmother told me once that she wrote it. I suppose she kept that a secret. So do I. Dunet named her stuffed bunny, Ceilia, after her. My lips tug up fondly at that.

I trace my fingers over the locket. My eyes grow clouded in the moment, my heart heavy, because I don't know who to keep closest now. By all means, it would be my sister. But it could be Myllia, and father is a choice—but probably not quite. Then there's Driena and Darnor ...

I look down at the ring on my right hand and hold it closer to my chest, smiling fondly as my eyes close a little.

Driena. I never really tell anyone what my ring is for. A special thing. I suppose it's the only piece of jewelry I allow myself to wear.

I sigh, casting my eyes out the circular window, barracks resting squarely in the distance—a constant reminder behind my head, something that calls to me. Sometimes it feels like a second home. Maybe not home, but a place where I feel at ease in my placement in the world.

I never considered myself a stressed person, but every so often, I find myself wanting to get out. Anything to calm my mind, but, really ... to see Myllia.

I close my eyes with a tingle in my spine. No. Not Dunet.

To be honest, I can't think about Dunet right now. When I do, it takes up all my time.

I don't have that time anymore. Sometimes I think I'm avoiding everything about home. I find time with Myllia and often Driena and Darnor instead, but more often in everything I now have to do. That means, at least a little time spent each day with Driena, and often Darnor. Truthfully, over the past few weeks, I haven't even gone home until after my family is asleep ... even my parents. My heart throbs to get back to them, but it's hard right now.

Father is probably worried.

I would think Dunet would be confused, but I don't know how to talk to her anymore.

She is stifling to think about. I just want to get away, as much as it pains me.

I normally like Wheln's office, but I just feel claustrophobic today.

The barracks stand imposingly on the border to the plains and the Kalltarris Mountains. It feels painted in the most beautiful way. Occasionally, I find myself staring at those mountains and fields when I'm too stressed and I need a break. It's hypnotic and soothing. Sometimes I forget what a beautiful place I live in. Sometimes Claralis is lonely and quiet, but it's beautiful in its solitude.

I pull my hand back from its splayed position. The floorboards creak as I stand and stretch.

While I do oversee the knights, paperwork takes up more time than I thought was possible. I knew that would be the case, and fortunately, I was and am very thorough in that regard. At noon though, it will be time for me to directly oversee the knights.

It can be draining to keep track of so many people, their progress, and remembering them, but I want to be a personable ruler.

So, I make my way down, even if it's early. Maybe it is a waste of my time, but I find that it's valuable. If anything, I think the only way to be a good ruler is to have genuine relationships with those you lead. I'm not their ruler, but their comrade. I'm their fellow knight, their fellow soldier. I've trained with them, gone through what they have, and faced the same expectations—at least, at first. That is what I want to create. I saw a kind ruler in my father, so I know I can be one too. Both him and Wheln set an example for me. Even mother set one ... Yes, I know that she most certainly did. I just wish I could recognize it without the sting of our soured relationship.

To defend something ... to genuinely defend it, means you care about it.

That is what they all showed me, and it's what I strive for. If anything, my dream to defend Dunet ... the person that drives me ... My dream is based around that ideal.

This place is like open air in my mind—welcoming, familiar, calming, and comfortable. It steadies me, gives me peace and purpose. It is a just place and a safe place, but that is only because of people like my father, like Wheln, and now, like me.

I turn out the door, my eyes falling on the expansive hall. High ceiling with crystalline chandeliers and the library opening warmly on either side, through the space between the massive columns. It's all shadowed alcoves and relaxing candlelight beyond here. I descend from the landing and I pass the towering azure blue banners on my left. The forest green carpet muffles my footsteps. It spreads over the polished wood steps. I exit the back side of the castle, at the tail end of the library.

The breeze is chilly and crisp under the tunnel-like canopy along the short path to the barracks. The wind passes over me lightly and a stream murmurs into a pond of lilies off to my right. My steps fall in their familiar, practiced cadence over the pebbles. The sky looks colder than it has been. Still a fairly light gray, but the darkest it has been. The light of the sun is already low to the horizon. Winter will come cold and dark this year, as it always has.

I set my teeth behind my pursed lip. That is far from the conditions I want, should the worst happen. Even if we remain untouched by war, winters lay our hearts in a place I would rather not have my soldiers or my people in during any danger. I can deal with it well enough, but I'm worried that other soldiers will waver. Everything good is scarcer in winter ... everything we need.

I hold myself upright, but all the while calm, as I pass towards the barracks that sit within the training fences, the windswept fields and solitary majesty of the Kalltarris Mountains in the background. Other knights dot the scene, wearing silver armor with highlights in Claralis' azure blue and forest green. Some knights fight one-on-one, some in formation, a few patrol the barrack wall and the castle walls, and some sit together on breaks in the greenery by the castle wall behind me, studying or socializing with one another. A few observe or hone their weapons.

I walk past Tenor and Lysis, a small group gathered around them behind the practice fence.

Lysis seems to see me, looking up with a nod—amethyst eyes, creamy complexion, and dark-red, nearly black hair, with light freckles and a lithe, springy form.

I nod back, my posture remaining solid. I don't think I can ever get used to this.

Tenor—messy brown hair, soft, but hardened face, deep blue eyes, lightly tanned skin, and a wiry, muscled frame—looks back and stumbles, to which I almost sigh and cover my face. But I do feel bad about his reaction when he sees me.

Unfortunately, people will always view me as their Commander, no matter what I went through with them. I suppose it doesn't help that I was studying under Wheln. I think everyone knew it would be me who would be commander.

I roll my eyes inwardly. Everyone knew, except for me, of course. And I was oblivious that they knew.

Or, at least, I avoided their praise and suggestions at all costs. I never knew what to do with it, except to brush it off casually.

No, someone else may become commander. It doesn't have to be me, just because I'm studying under Wheln.

How could I blind myself to the obvious?

I narrow my eyes back on Lysis and Tenor's fight, focusing on their every movement.

Lysis stabs fluidly, and Tenor side steps.

His footwork is good, but not fast enough. Her sword grazes his wrist. Then, he pivots and sweeps at her legs.

She brings her sword down to block, twists her wrist and drives it forward. Tenor steps back and twists his arm away. Her sword meets the spot where he would be. He pivots, before aiming his sword at her exposed side.

She drops away from his sword and lets his weight carry him forward, positioning herself to drive home the would-be fatal blow. His eyes go wide, but he stays composed at the end of the match.

Lysis braces herself to get up. Tenor helps her onto her feet. They shake hands.

Tenor seems bright enough, despite his loss. His eyes are keen, steady.

I look on with a satisfied smile.

I admire their quick thinking, even if a few things came out imperfect.

I would hate to be harsh.

It's still my job, though, to see this through. If something should happen, then I need to train them as best as I can.

I feel calm as Driena steps up beside me. "I can tell that you think the same as me, Liela." Her intelligent, silver-flecked, river blue eyes skim my face, her dark hair held past her delicate features in a ponytail. Her words are gentle, yet serious. "I like them as much as you do," she sighs out. "And they're good. I think we both just worry. I could nitpick it all day and I would probably be harsher than you." Her smile lightens. "I respect that about you. You balance me out—like my sister in arms."

"Thank you, Driena. Yes. I just … I think until I have some grasp of what's going to happen … that might help to put my mind at ease."

Her gaze meets mine. "Did you still want to go through with today's training?"

I look at the walls. "It's better than waiting."

"Liela." Driena meets my gaze with a pronounced weight. "Everything will be all right. Just know that I'll be by your side."

"I know, I can't let it show *so clearly* …" My smile spreads. "Thank you, Driena. I'll count on your support. I wish I could say that I wasn't afraid."

"And I would always say that you care too much and worry far more than you should."

I roll my eyes. "As you always do."

She motions to the walls with an upturn of her chin. "We should get started. It won't do you any better to dwell on it." She turns around, meeting my gaze clearly. "Liela, you are the only one who could've been commander. There was a reason it wasn't me. Just remember: I know you'll succeed." She turns her eyes away, her voice unwavering. "It's better this way. No matter what I say, I never doubted you."

I feel a slight shiver along my spine, then my smile turns grim. I feel like I should say something, but I don't know how to process that. She's by my side. That's all that matters. I know she's wrong that it only could've been me. I don't doubt myself, but I know she put in just as much effort

I try my best to let her words raise me.

For she is my star-soul.

I enclose the ring on my hand—it's slipped onto my right ring finger. A silver band with an engraved cluster of stars that seem to dance when you reangle it. That ethereal dance soothes me like a beacon of light in a dark abyss.

In Claralis' custom, a star-soul symbolizes a chosen sister. The traditional wedding band would be worn on the left ring finger, but a star-soul would be worn on the right, symbolizing an unbreakable bond of chosen sisters, those who always support each other and who would connect themselves in the stars throughout one's life and into death.

I thought it almost too sentimental for Driena, but I know she's soft at heart, even if her heart is firmer than mine.

I still haven't told Dunet about my star-soul.

As much as I publicly call Dunet my sister, Driena is just as much my sister as Dunet is.

She will always be my equal. I look up to her, despite our ranks.

Always. Even when I say we're equals.

A Memory of Star-Souls ~ Liela & Driena

Driena stares at me intently, her youthful eyes flaring, black hair I always thought was so pretty lashing in the wind, the silver and blue of her eyes flashing like lightning. She stands out before me on the wall, the sparse plain and the cold of the Kalltarris mountains standing in the gray-gold of morning, frozen in time. Driena is lit in a soft harshness that calls out to me, the stark still of dawn connecting our hearts.

She extends to me a ring: a silver band with a cluster of stars that dance in the space between us, beckoning me to reach her.

A ring for star-souls, sisters in the stars.

My mind is frozen, but I reach for her regardless. I know this is something special.

This is our moment from which we will tie our souls.

And I would lean on her.

We would lean on each other.

Forever.

A sacred vow of sisters.

I smile to her, caught up in a world with only us.

And she smiles back in a flame that connects us.

Her smile is soft under its hard resolve that gives me drive.

It was never *just* Dunet.

It was Driena too.

And she guides me, so I will not be a lost girl; because she knows that is not who I am. And while Dunet gave me purpose, Driena drives me forever forward.

Star Souls of the Present ~ Liela

Our eyes connect across that glorious chasm.

Her dark hair flies over her violet and silver armor, gleaming with purpose and poise across the still tide before a storm.

She faces me with all the grace of an angel about to rip the world apart.

Honed grace. A sharp steel as direct as the morning sun behind her.

She gives me a nod, turning to her archers—with mock arrows, of course, padded and harmless.

But she waits as I tap my fingers over the wall, scanning the tide of her mock army.

She knows I play things safe. I won't send out counter troops or surprise attacks. I don't like the thought of risking others for something like that. I would feel like I would be throwing them away.

But I don't know where she'll strike. She'll attack one of my weaknesses, but which one?

With a ruptured shout, I hear the alarm from the wall over to my right.

My eyes stay trained on her for a moment, and I beckon to a scout, watching their every move as I do, hand resting lightly on the pommel of my sword.

Courtney solutes. Braided, coarse hair, dark, angular face, gray eyes, and mottled white-gray-brown riding clothes—the closest thing to blend into the winter landscape.

I frown back at the battlefield. It's now too risky not to send scouts.

My brow creases as Driena leaves and takes her mock second. My lip creases and I bite down on it.

It must be bait.

Honestly, I feel like having Driena as a mock commander upsets my judgement. I'm overthinking her moves.

But still …

I shake my head and give the order aloud to reposition, then say to Courtney, "Take a small party and I'll leave a quarter of us just outside the wall, in case of an ambush."

She nods and turns with a flick of her eyes, step settling in a purpose that grows as she walks.

I purse my lips. A real siege would be chaos and fear.

I could never risk an escape route without that overwhelming grip shredding at my doubts—of a slaughter.

We would have to ration and keep everyone in a safe place.

The siege would have to be quick and soon.

We're too important to not receive aid eventually, if correspondence dropped indefinitely.

Nevertheless, there are too many variables that I can't account for.

Driena is agile in her planning … Not that that's what I'm worried about long-term.

For I can counter an enemy.

What I need most is to get everyone in the spirit of *knowing* we can win.

That, we can protect.

I find myself at the heart of the mock battle, frost and thin snow slipping at my movements over the battlements, something I can only grit my teeth at, and direct my archers to the meticulous progress of Driena's troops.

Everyone is calm in her command.

I bite my lip ... She is a formidable opponent, pushing just enough between calm and purpose.

It's then when I hear the counter attacks ringing simultaneously through the frozen air.

I narrow my eyes. Most of her forces are here.

But her generals are gone ... And with them, probably a party specializing in stealth and close combat.

I signal Elisa and Natasha. "Elisa, take the left ... And Natasha, the right."

Elisa nods, parched white hair streaming, blue eyes meeting mine as she turns. Natasha—hazel eyes, curled brunette hair, and light tan skin—nods and looks to her soldiers.

"Bring a fifth each and we'll hold the rest here," I say, ending the order.

I turn back to the wall. This may not be an accurate siege, but there's more to a siege than battle. Planning for time is what matters most—for distribution and storage and harboring all our spirit to hold out through it all.

We can do this, for it's necessary ... But as knights, we can do more than fight.

As relatively short as I anticipate this to be, if they hit us hard, instead of waiting us out and starving us, then we will need this.

I count on them rushing for a surprise on our country, Mathar. I count on the siege not being drawn out, which could either be what we need, or something that dooms us. For we can hold out, but in doing so, that will strain our resources, especially in winter.

Otherwise, everything theoretically is pointless.

But aide will take at least a week, and we have no word.

I catch Driena's steady, but satisfied grin as one of the siege towers—of sturdy wood and iron—makes it past the archers and hooks the wall.

The objective is to take half of one of our forces, or we surrender, assuming our opponent will be generous. I want to trust that.

With our forces spread strategically, I move to meet the second oncoming ladder with my sword at the ready.

I flawlessly dodge a sword drive from Eneir, and I step in, rendering him out of the fight.

One enemy down, I take a step back and consider my next move. The ladders are metal, so fire wouldn't work to destroy them. The only thing we can do is break them or toss them off the wall.

I meet another slash. Elli's turquoise eyes stare at mine—it takes me a moment to sort through faces, but even now, I do my best to remember her. I reposition with focus, catching the next overhead swipe. She wears herself out, and I take the opportunity to arch my sword and step to the side, keeping to the end of her reach. She deflects my attack, but her balance is chipping away. As she strikes again, I let her balance fall and move to a lower slash, catching her legs and rendering her out.

In a moment, the rest of Driena's forces pull back, leaving just the archers and those on the wall to keep us occupied.

I remain calm, motioning for the phoenix-red haired Rela to take half our forces to reinforce.

I sharpen my gaze at what's before me. Soon, I will have to join the tide.

But my thoughts rush past in the heat of it all ... Because Driena is the one I face.

Maybe it's stupidity, or the heat of the moment, but I stand to face her, sending the last orders to Ren and Vela to keep the rest here. Then, I step forward to face her.

Her eyes keep me in a trance as her sword traces at her side with grace. She brings her sword up ...

And I strike—a mocking blow, as I switch the direction, then move back into a defensive position.

She's meticulous—every blow carries meaning, and a message.

I try to keep the rest of the battle in my eyes, but for once, I let my blood sing and everything get away from me, even as I chide myself for it. Driena sings to me, and I let her. I know I'm being reckless.

Her sword comes up against mine again and I stumble, gritting my teeth and twisting our swords to break free. I move for a quick diagonal cut.

Her wrist is like lightning, and she blocks it, eyes singing.

I grin, beside myself with recklessness. Driena is one of the few who can do this to me—upset my normal composure.

However, I snap myself out of it in an instant, getting more careful. To defeat her, I must chip away at her flawless movements, as she's meeting me, blow for blow.

Until she twists, eyes flaring, and I catch the move. I react instinctively, my sword posed at her breast. The match is over.

Her eyes meet mine, soft and serious. We share in our admiration for one another, this sisterly connection between us.

I won this and my chest can't help swelling with pride.

But then, I hear the sound of Driena's horn of victory. My heart falls.

Driena won. I lost.

She smiles apologetically. "Sorry, Liela, but you put up a good fight."

I close my eyes. My shoulders fall as I breathe out my nose.

I focused too much energy on my battle with Driena. I got distracted. Maybe she would've won anyway? I know she probably would've today … But the fight would've been much closer had I been focused on the right thing. Like our personal battle, it would've rested more equally.

I smile again, regardless. It's a grim line. Maybe I let this happen, but I can avoid it later, when the real thing … if the real thing happens. At least I know that Driena will not be my enemy.

I meet Driena after we regroup, a resigned light in my eyes. Driena already senses my thoughts—she knows me better than I know myself.

"Do not fault yourself, Liela. You did what you could. It's unlikely that we'll have any advantage. You told me yourself that you wanted me to take a larger force. We will plan and practice. We both know that there's much more to worry about than this."

My eyes skim the soldiers. There's exhaustion in their eyes and their breathing is thick. "I'm worried that it's too much."

"You know that we can only focus on so much. You're doing what you can with what you have, Liela."

I sigh, meeting her eyes. "You performed breathlessly today."

"Liela ..." She halts her words. "So did you."

"But I should have seen you coming." I brush it off, still feeling that discomfortable prickle on my skin at my lack of foresight and focus.

She meets my eyes intently, a stirring of warmth behind them. "You get too emotional when you fight me directly."

My breath catches. I don't want to admit it.

"What I think ... is that you should switch us out sometimes."

I sigh, stubborn guard falling to her suggestion. "You may be right. You catch me off balance when I feel that I should know your every move."

"And that is the only reason you overthink it, Liela." She looks back at me, eyes reflected her subtle humor.

I stiffen in the moment, agreeing with her, while not catching her soft tone.

"That was a joke, Liela."

I correct myself impulsively because I should be able to read Driena's every meaning. "I know." I pause, then raise my eyes to the sky, now grinning, just a little tightly. "I frustrate myself sometimes."

"Liela, how about we cool down for a while? The lord suggested it." I can hear the jubilant pitch at the end of her voice, that probably no one else would recognize ... except for maybe Darnor. It took me a while to recognize her compassion for him for what it was. I still have trouble telling the difference between the looks of friendship and romance, but I've decided that they're in love. Or, well, Driena told me when she was drunk—I won't tell her that though, because I don't want to embarrass her, but I would've never figured it out by myself—and after finding out she liked him, I won't let myself not be pushy, because I want that for them more than anything. Especially for her.

However, today's different.

"Driena." I look at her meaningfully. "As much as I like him, sometimes I just want some girl time. Just with you." I breathe in and shake my head. "He isn't the same ... I know I see you more, but if I'm being honest, you mean a little more to me."

Her steady eyes meet mine. "I can put him off for us."

"And frustrate him." I nudge her with a knowing gleam to my eyes.

"I would say that he would hardly care."

"I would hardly think so, but, hopefully, he takes a hint." I quirk my lips. "Really, though ..." I turn serious. "I do want to see him. I never want to alienate him. I just need him in a different way ..."

"Liela, you know how obvious your intent is?"

Of course. I close my eyes. Everything always seems too plain to everyone else, except me—especially to Driena. Even when I think I'm being subtle, somehow it's crystal clear.

"You don't even need to say that, Liela. We both know what type of person you are." Her smile is kind and so very deep.

"You see everything from me too easily, Driena. It's disconcerting ..."

"No less than your honesty."

I stare at her for a moment, letting that settle in, then look back at the aftermath of our knights dispersing, unable to find an answer to that statement. I look back to her. "I know that just as you do ... I do need a rest."

"As I say, Liela: You go too far out of your way for your own good. Sometimes I wonder if you know what it feels like to relax."

I bite my lip, then close my eyes. I know that this is the only way to keep my mind honed—keep myself from losing it. I nod. "Then, let's catch a quick break." I grin, seeming to stumble into a proper response to her teasing.

"Afterward, I suppose I will go back to overworking myself …"

"I expected nothing less." She falls into step next to me, keeping me steady as we walk forward in sync.

Caroline Sophia Hamel

Dunet

"Dunet!" Lily bounds up beside me, seawater eyes set on me. She holds her basket under her arm, the other swinging at her side. My eyes always drift to her basket with curiosity. It's winter, so it seems an odd time for one. She stands out—pigtails and dress apart from most of the other students—but she keeps to herself mostly.

She goes a bit stiff as she gets closer.

"Lily!" I pull on a smile.

She laces her fingers in front of her. "Mind if we talk some?"

"I don't mind ..." I want to shrink away again. Her gaze is off-putting.

"The weather is so nice out, don't you think?"

I laugh hollowly, mind searching for something to say, but not really finding anything. "You like gray?"

"Don't you? It's comforting."

My mouth goes dry. Can she read me? "It is ..."

"Dunet." She swings her basket side-to-side. "I can't help but wonder when I look at you ..." She shakes her head. "Forget it."

My mind blanks. "What do you mean?"

"Nothing." But her eyes are far too piercing for her to mean that. They send a shiver up my spine. She glances at me and smiles in a way that twists my insides. Part of me likes her. Part of me doesn't. Part of me hates myself for thinking that. "Maybe I'm a little crazy?"

I take a moment to regroup my thoughts. "You're not crazy." I reassure her with a warm-enough smile.

"I know." Her voice is a little meek. "Dunet, I wanted to do something with you."

"Okay …" I keep my voice level, but my hands shake a little and I want to run. I know that, like how it is with every other person I've met, no matter how much people seem to like me, there's a gap between us that I can't close. I can't relate to others.

Sometimes, I don't even feel like a person. I can never communicate how I want to and by now … that just makes friendship painful. I feel far away, even when I'm so close. In a group, I'm let in, but can't function within it. People never see me. They see my image and only that. People like me because I seem nice; because I seem carefree and bright; because I never do anything wrong; because I'm perfect at seeming perfect. I'm not kind or carefree. I'm not bright. I'm nothing.

Why should Lily be any different? And yet, something keeps telling me to run. I make sure to put on my brightest smile. "I would be happy to!"

She narrows her eyes for a moment, then smiles back. "I like the outdoors! Although, I don't think I'm much of a people person," she stumbles. It seems like she's forcing herself to hold eye-contact. I look at the space just behind her.

"Well, you seem nice to me!"

"Of course, I do. You like everyone. Still ..." she muses, placing her fist under her chin. "Forget I said that. Say, if it were summer, we could go berry picking. Oh, I do long for summer ... You ever been to the forests near the horizon?"

I shake my head.

"Probably not a good idea right now." She brings her mouth into another smile. "I like you. I won't tell you why yet. I just do. Say, two weeks from now I'll have plenty of time." She turns away slightly. "I have trouble saying why though. Something about you seems ... safer."

I'm caught off guard for a moment, realizing she asked a question. "Yes!" I squeak.

She laughs suddenly and stares at me. "Are you lonely?" she asks quietly.

I swallow.

"Don't worry about it, but I'd be prepared is all." She shrugs and turns on her heel, basket swinging. "See ya!" She waves over her shoulder, then runs off.

I wave back, mind utterly jumbled.

I feel like I'm in a trance as I turn away.

A Fragile Fairytale

Liela

I find it a struggle to leave Driena for Dunet.

I don't like to say that.

But Driena just makes me feel calm.

And Myllia makes me feel fuzzy and free.

With Dunet, everything comes back, and I can barely hold myself together or see anything clearly.

How do I deal with that?

Yet, how could I think of her like this?

Like a burden.

She's not one.

She never was and I never want her to be.

She was always that light I protected … Not something I wanted to run from.

I close my eyes, collecting myself.

There's no point in overthinking everything. I want to be calm for her and to be there for her. I just never thought that it would be this hard.

I make my way up into our tower, glancing into her room, with painted doves and flowers, white flowing sheets, and still-blowing curtains, Ceilia, her fluffy-white stuffed bunny, set with care on the bedsheets.

Her lessons are long since over.

I feel a tenseness leave me, but I should ... I still want to look for her. I know it would make sense to miss her, but in truth, I really hesitate to find her, although my thoughts scream at me to do so.

On instinct, I know that I should look for her in the stables, and I make my way down the spiral steps, through the large hall, the moderate milling of people starting to fill under the domed ceiling in late morning.

I take the short flight of steps and cross the neatly trimmed grass to the stables, feet crunching with a disturbed rhythm over the frozen dew. Its wood and iron trimming and the pointed and inward curving roof remains a familiar sight, and a haunting one. I can never shake those memories, still sharp and fresh in my mind, of how much everything hurt that day.

The close, dusty air swirls in a gentle stillness, as I creak open the door, disregarding my hesitation. Soft beams of light shine through hazy shadows in the hay- and dust-filled expanse.

My smile lifts as I see her saddling Eriena, right hand stroking the horse as she whispers in her ear, her words too intimate for me to hear.

"There you are, Dunet!"

Her smile lights to see me, but it's like a shadow of her old smile, only glancing off her eyes. Her eyes seem to pale, even with her held smile and even though they stay on mine ...

My hands shake. I breathe in deeply through my nose and hold my eyes up.

I tell myself that it's only natural, as she brings her hands behind her back, as if to hide them. Did she always do that?

I soften my voice, even as it sounds brittle in my own ears. "How are you?" My question feels so off and jagged from my lips ... I don't know where everything went.

"Fine." It slips from her mouth like it's caught on her tongue—dry and forced, and after only a moment, she goes back to darting her eyes.

How did I never notice how much she holds in?

Why was I never paying attention?

"I had lessons with Halfern for a few hours. He says I am progressing well." Her eyes meet mine, then she ducks her head. I swear, I catch them shine a little, but I don't know if it's my imagination. Then her voice drops, and she shuffles her feet. "I am doing my best to focus." She stumbles, glancing up from her downcast eyes. "I enjoy lessons more than I used to ..." She pulls in a breath, lacing her words with the childish grin that she should have. "Although, they are still boring without you." I know that smile, and it really is genuine.

A smile touched with sunshine.

My heart leaps. "Maybe I could stop by one of them?" My heart races. I wonder whether it's guilt or excitement. I just know that I want to latch onto her brightness.

"Will you?" she asks, heels rising from the ground. The air seems to dance around her, and my breath catches. Everything seems to pull together, latching onto a flower in sunlight.

This is my Dunet. This is my sister.

My smile creases.

Whatever I can do to protect her smile, then I will do it.

I don't know how, but I know this is something. A start to …

I don't know what.

Whatever it is, I won't let this moment slip away from me …

From us.

I will give her what she needs, even if I don't know what that is.

My heart settles, and my mind stops its racing thoughts enough to clear. "When I find the time, I promise I will."

She beams in her familiar way, one that lights my heart. She stands on her tiptoes, whirling her head in the direction of Eriena, streams of white lifting in the air that now seems so much fuller. "Could we go riding?"

My smile settles, my heart caught on a gentle breeze in the moment. "I have time for it now. Unfortunately, only a little over an hour, but it's something." I stumble over the last part, knowing that my schedule would eventually call me away from her.

"Let's get as much in as we can!" Dunet says with a slight shrill note. She turns away to Eriena. I'm sure she was hoping for more, but I can't express how much my heart lifts to have even a little time to spend with my sister.

"Yes, Dunet …" I cradle her in a smile. "I will stay as long as I can." I move over to Vel, patting her, letting just the barest strain show on my lips. "Good girl, Vel. Thank you." I turn around, making sure Dunet isn't looking, and meet Vel's eyes meaningfully. I wonder how similar Eriena is for Dunet as Vel is for me. Sometimes the tension in my eyes would show after a long day to her.

But it took Myllia to really let it out.

Vel—she's strong and proud and wise and gentle … Sometimes I don't appreciate that. I feel like I don't even have to say anything to let her know …

To let her know …

My mind blanks for a moment.

I blink, regaining my train of thought.

66

I am grateful that she is my companion.

I blink again, remembering Dunet behind me; what I'm doing here. I want to be myself with her.

Vel's hooves meet the delicate white of snow, gradually hardening and building next to Eriena, Dunet saddled on her.

I breathe in, closing my eyes, before opening them to gentle white.

But Dunet isn't there. She isn't looking at me.

She leans over Eriena, looking into the distance as she murmurs in Eriena's ear.

I feel a throb in my throat, already unable to keep hold of her hand, as she walks too far away to reach.

I pull on the reins, halting Vel. Ghosts of white flurries hide her.

She looks back, eyes cracked, then a smile twists onto her face and her eyes light ... Before it lets go to brightness ... and the sun flits behind her ...

She seems to reach for me ... a loose string through blurry flakes. All I can see is her, yet I don't feel anything.

I reach for her, my mind murky, even as it relaxes in this reprieve.

Caroline Sophia Hamel

I realize my eyes are wet—the snow blurs more than it should—and I reach up to wipe at them, pulling on a fragile smile.

Who is she?

And what am I doing wrong?

I can only blindly stumble forward, wanting to believe that my steps never faltered to begin with ...

Because I don't know when they did ... And I'm too afraid to try fixing them.

A Harsh Hope

Liela

I swipe at Driena, my sword homed in all the wrong ways and my mind pulsating, out of the moment. I bite on my lip, gritting my teeth against my intrusive thoughts, but it does me no good, because I can barely keep my breathing relaxed.

Driena predictably meets my every blow without flinching—her dark hair whips at her face and her eyes narrow thoughtfully at my rushed strokes.

I take another hurried blow and Driena takes a slow step back, bringing her sword up.

My forehead creases in frustration. My vision blurs, but I drive all my effort into each stroke.

Then Driena lowers her sword and stares at me intently. "Liela." Her voice is soft, but she contains so much weight in her gaze.

My breath comes out heavy and I try not to bite my words. "What is it?" My spine is rigid though, and my sword arm is heavy.

Driena brings her sword back into her scabbard and crosses her arms. Her eyes seem to burn, like she knows my every secret. But below that harshness, I know that she's trying to be comforting. "Liela, you are off balance, and you're putting all your energy into strikes that I think you know won't work. I know you when you fight, and I just know that something is bothering you."

It feels draining to even stand here right now. If I could collapse, I know that I would. "I'm just a bit tired." I try tugging on a smile, but I know that Driena can read right through it. I draw my sword back up anyway, a wariness creeping into my eyes, as if that will guard me from the sharpness of Driena's intensity ... As if she didn't already know me well enough.

Driena's eyes harden, and she taps her foot, her voice slicing against the weak walls of my mind—they slowly collapse to her every word. "Are you?" Her voice bites against the silence. She pauses for a moment, and I quiver tensely. "Liela?" she inquires, her tone lightening.

I know that I want to let her in. Maybe I need to?

I let my eyelids close as I sigh ever so slightly. The urge to let go tempts me so.

Darnor clears his throat kindly from the sidelines, and only now do I remember that he's there. I turn my eyes to him, resigned that they can both read me easily. I know what's coming.

"Liela." His eyes are clear and empathetic, like he's telling me to lower my guard. "You are clearly more than tired." He pauses. "Is everything all right between you and Dunet?"

I know that they both know the answer without me having to say anything. After all, I know that he has been worried for her since the beginning, and Driena may not say so herself, but I know that she is too.

I wish that I'd listened to them both back then, because maybe I could have helped her? Maybe, with their help, I wouldn't feel so lost in this? Maybe I could've given Dunet the support I don't know how to give her now?

I take a deep breath. "Sorry. Both of you." I press my fingers to my temples, trying to relieve all the pressure I feel building up, pressing in on me from all sides. My walls are hard for most things, but when it comes to Dunet, it's like they aren't there. Transparent. "It's just … I failed as an older sister. I failed Dunet." My voice is falling too, no energy left to keep it steady.

There's no point in hiding my feelings anymore.

I've opened the floodgates already, and it's like I can never close them or satisfy them once that's done. I thought that it would be enough to have Myllia to talk to, but that's not all that I want … Really, it's like I never wanted to hide anything from *anyone* … But it's only now that I realize I *was hiding*. The smallest things I did to protect Dunet and not harm her—they all stacked up to this.

What else is there that I never realized was there? How much did I decide not to see until now, or still don't? I feel panicked from not wanting to know all the truths that are there.

Caroline Sophia Hamel

Until now, I hadn't realized just how much of a burden they were. If only my fears were not rushing at me, like a choppy ocean wave during a terrible storm.

I know Dunet is still there, as I knew her … I let myself truly see her, but at the same time … I feel like I let her go. I should feel relief. I should feel happy that I'm finally trying to understand who she's becoming. But … am I?

All I feel is an empty pit. It was so much easier when I was ignorant, even when the connection I treasured was really a veil I wore over my eyes. I wanted to be ignorant and imagine Dunet was the same. The Dunet I knew was a fantasy I wrote to fulfill my own desires, not hers.

I was truly never there. Neither for her, nor with her. If anything, she was there for me; she took away my stress and fear. I never let her reach for her own future. I made it up for her, thinking I knew what was best for her and what she wanted and needed from me. She deserves better than that, and I want to try. For the first time, I am truly trying, or I hope that I am …

"You didn't fail her, Liela," Darnor says with a calm, slow voice, free from any doubt.

It makes me snap back to reality. I catch Driena sending him an affectionate look that touches at my heart, even if I pretend not to notice.

"You told me it was her choice and she made it." He stresses his words carefully, his eyes clear as he leans up from his position on the fence. "You told me you wanted that for her, when she was ready. And she is, Liela," he says, his voice drawing me into an unstable sense of clarity. "Liela, she might need help, but you *will* be there, and we both want to be there too."

My breathing comes out uneven and I close my eyes, trying to pull back my words that are all falling apart. "But I didn't … Not really," I say in barely a whisper, my heart sinking in defeat.

Dunet finally made her choice. If anything, I hoped she'd never make one.

Driena breaks that haunting silence, taking a step forward and opening her arms, the hardness of her eyes drifting away at the edges. "Liela, you trust her. That's true, right?"

"Yes, it is." Of course, it is. Because what kind of a sister am I if I don't? But … maybe I don't? I meet the silver in Driena's eyes, and I know that I trust *her* like a sister. So, why can't I trust Dunet in the same way? Why can't I trust her with her own future?

Her voice sharpens again, her intent clear in every word. I always know she's like this because she only cares about my well-being. I know it sometimes hurts, but this is Driena. She never *wants* to hurt me, only tell me the truth she knows I need. "Liela, you came to terms with this. Am I right about that?"

It's not that simple. It never was and it never will be. "I don't think … that I ever can." If anything, I feel like I put up an act of acceptance at the stables—that I was all right with what she wanted and how she felt. All my emotions were so potent and real in the moment, and it's only now that it's truly settling in.

Darnor walks out from behind the practice fence, over to me, pleasant face and elegant hair exuding something familiar and calming. He places a hand on my shoulder and I smile back at him, a spark of fractured gratitude shining in my eyes.

Driena walks the remaining distance to me, her eyes clear of that icy intent; the kindness that was underneath it prevails. "Liela, you want her to trust you. You have to make the step. She wants to trust you. You are already halfway there. Talk to her like you did the other day." She looks at me with certainty. "That is all you need." She smiles and it stirs my heart. "It's all you ever needed. Just remember that she is living her own life now." Her gaze breaks for a moment, before her eyes look up to stare at me again, to lift me from this dark pit I've fallen into. "I had to remember that, too. And Liela ..." Her eyes are suddenly distant, shuttered. "It was also hard for me ..." I hear a harsh snap at the end of her sentence, and perhaps I am feeling a semblance of the pain she feels.

I search her expression and find the free smile has returned to her face. "I can carry on if you can, Liela."

It slips from my voice like a candle caught in a storm. "I'm scared," I murmur after several seconds, trying to put my words into something tangible. "I know you're right. Thank you. Both of you." I look between them.

Darnor nods to Driena and she steps forward, taking a breath in and embracing me. "Liela ... I'm sorry that I can't control myself sometimes, but I know everything will be fine, because I believe in you ..." Her voice catches. "To me, you are my sister, so keep trying for me. You both deserve that. You deserve better than what I went through. I know that I'm not perfect."

The moment feels so delicate, frozen in time and special. I whisper into her ear. "Thank you, Driena. I look up to you too, so I'll try. But Driena, I love you for everything you are."

I barely hear her voice, but it's as if I don't need to. "Because you are my star-soul."

"And everything makes a bit more sense with you, Driena. I think I would be lost without you."

She pulls away and glares at Darnor, and he expresses and easy grin. "You know that I'm glad to be included." He comes up to join us in a hug.

"It was your idea," she hisses.

His laugh rings sweetly. "I would just hate for it to end in anything depressing. In truth, I'm worried about Dunet. And Liela, I promise to talk to her for you."

I nod, my throat dry.

We pull apart and I smile at them with a smile that's just a bit more sure than I feel.

Driena says, "There's no use dwelling on what could've been. Even though I know you will, you can't change the past, Liela. We should get back to the session. Frankly, I'd like to see Darnor try his hand. A lord could use some exercise."

I roll my eyes and let out a freer laugh that melts into the air. "That is, if he even can!"

"Trust me, I don't want to. My lessons are hard enough as it is!"

"Don't give me that, Darnor," Driena snips.

"Oh, but I think the lord is right."

Darnor chuckles.

"Don't side with him, Liela. Remember?"

"I think I do. Don't worry, I'll leave him for you eventually."

Driena smiles at him tenderly. "You hear that, Darnor."

He steps back, leaning into the practice fence again. "I do."

My laugh comes out nearly raucous, as I bend over at the stomach. I actually get it, and I'm joyous at the thought of them together.

"What is it, Liela?" Darnor holds a twinkle in his eyes.

"It's just … I love you both. I really do! Fine, you can have each other! But Darnor, know that you're just tagging along like always!"

He winks. "Oh, I most definitely do!"

"Right." I roll my eyes and gesture beside me. I gesture beside me. "Then, will the two love birds duel?"

"Liela!" Driena's eyes jolt wide open.

"Driena, I wanted to say this in person, but I'm happy for you both."

"I … I know you are, Liela. I just …" She looks away, crossing her arms. "We are not together."

I roll my eyes again.

I'm glad I have both of them and Myllia to lean on. I never know what I would do without them.

And if I want Dunet to trust me, then I need to start talking to her directly. Everyone has been constantly telling me that, but all I wished for was ignorance.

I feel a shiver in my heart, because I don't *want* to do this.

But I tell myself it's not for me.

It's for Dunet. Everything is and everything always was. This is how it must be.

The Nightmares That Haunt Us

Liela

Dunet sits up from her white bedsheets, folded like veils of cloud, and she looks at me with boundless eyes of sapphire, the room misty in her wake. The starlight seems splayed behind her like a cradle that we sit in. My vision feels muddled, but through that, there's warmth. "Will you come back tomorrow, Liela?"

"No." I say, my voice passive and flat, my mind muted, even as my heart tries to flicker and burn. Yet, I can't shake myself to find her smile.

"Why not?" She cocks her head, waves of buttery hair hitting the sheets, the twinkling sparks in her eyes wavering, but not falling. Her face looks so rosy and innocent.

"Because I have so much more to do … And it's all for you." I settle my voice, but I can feel it suffocating me.

"It is?" Her voice is still bright, but there's something piercing to it and my chest starts to constrict.

"Yes," I say, but a flicker of gray wavers in my mind. Those lights are winking out, as I try to hold them and her here with me.

"So, I can't come?" Her sapphire eyes fall, her voice lost and far away, but still reaching for me, tugging for me … from a severing string …

"No, Dunet." My voice is too cold, too distant. "You need to understand that I'm doing this all for you." I turn my voice delicate and sure—a false conviction carries in the motionless air.

"But you're leaving me."

My stomach twists in silent agitation. "I am."

She cocks her head again. "But it's not *for* me. You're doing this for yourself, Liela ... Sister." Her face constricts, a harsh, wet stare set on me; one that she can barely hold. It's so close to breaking ...

Her look drives through my heart. I would rather die than feel this suffocating weight ... And as she disappears, I drop to my knees, shaking.

With the blink of my eyes, a mist of gray wraps my vision—to an ethereal courtyard, mists tickling its edges.

Dunet sits there in a bed of pure white flowers, turning her carefree gaze to me. I'm tugged towards her, and I see how her eyes reflect my smile.

"Liela!" she exclaims with a lofty peak to her voice that beckons me in its lightness. She rises from the vibrant flower bed, bounding over to me. "I missed you!" She brings her tiny arms around me, beaming up at me from her soft face with all the light in the world.

"I missed you too, Dunet!" I cast a blanketing look down at her, stroking back the messy strands of her buttery blonde hair.

She laughs, and it rings out in an echo. The world seems to dance around her in scattering color.

I release her with arms that suddenly feel heavy and empty, unable to move at my sides.

She bounds away, skipping, then twirls through the patches of coppery-gold leaves and the pure whites of the flowers. Then she turns back to me, her face haunted and the light fading from her eyes.

I realize, with a shaking catch of my heart, that I'm no longer reflected there; I'm merely a dull silhouette.

"Dunet." I try to keep the rising tension out of my voice. "What is it?"

She stares at me coldly, hollowly. "You did this to me, Sister."

Her eyes are dead.

And I'm frozen.

My breath catches and I try to formulate a response, choking on my words. My legs become unsteady; I stumble forward.

This isn't Dunet.

I did this.

"I love you, Dunet ..." It's all I can say, but I want to scream. Tears well in my eyes when I look at her distorted image.

Her eyes are empty, and she reaches for me pleadingly, all her light winked out … Gone. "Then come back …" It's so soft that it hardly reaches my ears, but I know that it would have been impossible not to hear.

Her voice enchants me, a fading innocence lacing her words, echoing in the hollows of my mind. I reach for her … but she's too far away.

My shriek cuts off as she fades into blackness …

I wake up screaming and desperately grasping for something, anything … to know that what I saw wasn't real. My tears break in a scattered sob, as I choke on them and try to hold on.

I hear the pad of Dunet's slippers as she peers in at me, holding Ceilia's fluffy white form in her arms. I do my best to hide my labored breathing, but I find my hand clutched to my chest. I force a broken smile through it all, but it's all still so vividly raw and poignant in my mind, no matter how close she is. And now, I almost don't want her here, as much as I need her.

"It's nothing, Dunet. Don't worry." I try not to wipe at my eyes, but there's no way I can hide how raw and fragile they are. My voice won't stop shaking. "You should be in bed," I soothe.

Her eyes flit away for a moment, then stay on me with hesitation—it's too direct for what I know.

"Was it about me?"

I hardly register her lips moving to those words. She knew already.

My heart breaks at her question, and I whisper, "Yes."

"Liela." Her eyes retreat and look past me—there's a shadow of moistness to them, but her voice is so steady. Far too steady. It hurts, wrapping around my lungs. "I'll be fine. I promise." Her voice is soft, sure ... yet distant.

My heart feels like breaking again at her maturity. I fail to hold it together, my features contorting, before I release a constricted sob. I bite down, trying to stop it, bringing my palms over my eyes, but I only cry more. I want so much to be there for her, but I can't even do that right now.

I can see Dunet staring at me with an unreadable expression. Her eyes fall, then pull back up—clear, even as the pale light of the moon fails to reach them.

She seems so calm.

I shut my eyes, feeling the soft touch of tears on my cheek. A moment later, I can feel her leaning into me, hugging me gently. "I will not go anywhere." Where did that steadiness come from? Where did my Dunet go?

Tentatively, I remove my palms from my eyes and wrap my arms around her small frame, my tears drying in streaks on my face. "You know, I'm proud of you. I never wanted this." Another sob comes out of me. "I really am sorry."

"Liela, you are the best sister I could ask for." Her voice is a whisper, but one that builds up, from wavering into clarity. Then that steadiness falls. "I ... You did everything for me."

I find myself clamping my jaw shut, to keep myself from breaking down further at those words.

She seems so small again; I want to bring her closer. "I am afraid too. It's okay though." She pulls on a strained smile.

"I know I shouldn't feel this way, Dunet. I have you right here."

I can feel her throat bobbing and I hold her closer. I stroke her hair back, turning to look into her eyes. "You are a beautiful little sister, you know that?"

She looks away from me.

I wipe the remaining tears from my face, holding her for several long minutes. She's tense, but I think I feel her body loosen for an instant. "I think that's enough for tonight." I pause. "Do you want to sleep here tonight?"

She nods into my shoulder, looking up at me with a bright, but wavering smile plastered on her dimpled cheeks.

I draw in the warmth I want to feel—a bittersweet affection shows in my eyes. "Dunet. I really am proud. I want you to be whoever you decide to be. Do you think you can do that?"

She nods after a moment, even if her beautiful sapphire eyes mist over.

I release a breath, smiling again. "Good. I'll still be here, Dunet. You will never have to do this alone."

I hope that's enough.

Dunet

I burrow into her, seeking the darkness and her warmth—and her words, as elusive and distant as they are.

Every word stung, but for the wrong reasons.

Because I don't deserve them—I want to hide from them, even as I want to grasp them.

I am the one who changed.

The one who is selfish.

I'm no longer doing this for her, but for myself.

I've always been selfish.

And I don't want to see Liela cry for me.

I wish I could stay the person she needs.

I miss that person, too. She presses on me like a forgotten, soft kiss ... But she isn't here. She's just a mournful memory, and I wonder if she even existed in the first place.

Now that I know Liela will always be here, my world still feels unstable. I still think I'm alone. The edges of darkness scream at me and I hide from them.

The world scares me. I scare me.

I hate myself for how much I'm hurting Liela. It bites at me like all the coldness I keep locked away and left to build inside me.

But I promise … I promised myself that I would do this all for her; that I would take up this burden, so she wouldn't have to.

I must, or else I have nothing. Nothing but cold.

For the first time, this is something that I want to do.

This is something that I will do.

Not just for my sister, but for me.

Because I want this for myself.

And I will move towards that future on my own.

…

With Liela by my side …

Because even now, I need her here to let me know that everything will be all right.

I still need her.

Maybe it's selfish, but I think I always will be.

A Chill of the Heart

Dunet

Did winters always feel this cold?

I wonder if they did.

For some reason, I find the cold comforting. It doesn't constrict me, demanding that I find warmth. Because of this, I seek out the cold.

I am going to places where no one will find me.

When I seek someone out, it is for my own selfish wishes to find love and to pretend for people.

That is all that I'm good for—pretending to be this person who brings temporary happiness to others.

A shiver makes me snap my back up straight. I stare out at the solitary courtyard in which I hide, wishing I was anywhere but.

I wish I could be a girl from one of Liela's stories.

They are brave and kind ... Not like me.

I wish that I could forget the world.

Go away.

I want everything ...

While I want to lose it all.

My nails scrape at the stonework in the crease of the wall, resting there behind a courtyard fountain, ivy shielding me from the gazes above, a few scattered flurries of snow making their way through the ivy and bushes.

I love small spaces, where I can hide.

I find them comforting. Cradling. The only warmth I have …

But I can never hide from myself.

That is what I want to hide from most.

What I *need* to hide from.

Because my nails want to rake at my mind. They want to sink into my heart … Inside, it hurts so much.

I pull my knees up, my hand falling from the wall … scratch marks are now there, like deep gouges in skin.

I tilt my head back and spot a patch of blue, so far away.

I reach for it, but only feel the hollowness carve deeper into my soul. It has not consumed me yet, and I don't really know when it started.

I frown, tilting my head back, the breeze just barely reaching me.

Then, I laugh.

Dry and brittle and cracking.

I'm still myself. Every time I feel empty ... I tell myself that I will push forward for Liela.

It feels so ironic. We're like polar opposites ... And somehow, we're the same.

While she is selfless ... All for me ...

I am selfish ... For her, and for myself.

To Stitch When You Want to Break

Liela

I feel a shudder and a shaking of my hand.

I can do this.

I've always done what I thought I needed to do, and I was always ready.

But why does this scare me?

I take my strides through the musty lighting, rare sunshine streaming through the hallway windows. I keep my head up, but this shaking won't ease.

What is she going through? Is it all settling in?

I know Halfern is kind to her, but I know now that what she's learning must be weighing on her.

I know that she never dreamed of this.

I know she never wanted this.

And I can't help going back to thinking that it's all my fault.

I try shaking my head. After all, I now know that she's resolved to do this, and I don't want to take her choice away from her, because she has never expressed herself like this.

It scares me.

That look that burns me—her eyes focused and not hers.

I tell myself again and again that that can be part of her, and the other parts must still be there.

I never wanted to disappear from her life, but I'm tempted, and just thinking that makes me want to scream.

Because I keep remembering that I *based myself* on a fairytale of her.

I pause outside the room, then my heart jumps—I'm at my destination already.

Why do I feel numb suddenly?

No, the numbness fades. It was there for only a passing moment.

I breathe out, close my eyes, and open the door. My gaze settles on Halfern as he is reciting to Dunet.

She pauses, nearly jumping, and turns her eyes to me, smile twitching at her lips. Mine stretches, as if pulled by a thread.

"Ah, Liela." Halfern creases his brow at me.

"Halfern, I hope that I'm not intruding."

"Certainly, you are not, and I think that Dunet is happy to see you."

I nod to him with a smile. "Thank you for allowing me to come."

He nods several times with a knowing smile and turns back to Dunet.

I wave to Dunet encouragingly and she breathes in, seeming to slow down and turn back to Halfern. Her eyes look straight forward, and her posture stiffens.

I feel a jab at her obvious discomfort, but know it's not anything against me. She must be just as nervous. And I hope that I look as confident and supportive as I'm trying to come off.

"Shall we continue?" Halfern turns his gentle blue eyes to her, his wrinkled face inviting and kind.

Dunet nods, squirming in her chair, but she meets his eyes with purpose.

Halfern casts an approving look at me. It settles my heart a little at how at ease he is with Dunet and to have me here to watch her.

"Now, can you tell me why Villenas is an important location?" His eyes are prying, but soft in that nudge, arms relaxed on the desk before him.

Dunet screws up her face and I can't help thinking how much younger it makes her look.

She draws her answer out slowly, as the information seems to dawn on her. "It's important because it's a school where everyone can go to learn."

"Correct. Villenas was created as neutral territory, as a place of learning. It's a place to gather knowledge together—to learn and grow together, so that we can mend and accept one another. That is what it's meant for and what it was created for."

Dunet seems to take a moment to gather the information. "It sounds special."

"Yet, it's highly contentious. It's a place fought over in regional influence and the opportunity to attend is just as contested. It's more a symbolic gesture, if you will, and it's become a place of prestige, contrary to its original intention. Theoretically, anyone can attend."

Dunet frowns, her eyes seeming further away.

"Villenas remains technically neutral. Whether or not that is the case remains debated. It's a symbol of what should be, but nothing is perfect in this world. The certainty is that it still stands."

"You mean, it's not really fair?"

"Yes, that's what is now strongly believed." Halfern's voice is calm and consoling, his patience immeasurable, and I respect that.

"Now, can you tell me the significance of Iro?"

"I think that it was an empire?" She cocks her head slightly.

"That's correct. It was a joining of the countries of the north—an alliance, of sorts, under Arathulen. There are several countries on that have had withstanding conflicts with Mathar, our country." Halfern pulls out a large map rolled up next to his desk, unfolding it and pointing to several countries as he speaks. "Arathulen was able to bring them together in a united cause—Arathulen, Hazolhern, Helsor, and Malos. And Mathar allied with Juleck, Aryul, and Clilsa. Thus, came the last great war, resulting in the dissipation of Iro and Mathar becoming the greatest military power on this continent, gaining a following of influence that has been difficult to surpass. Can you tell me why the Iro alliance formed?"

Dunet shakes her head vigorously, after a pause.

"With power comes influence and with influence comes tragedy. Mathar and Arathulen have always been world powers. The other countries joined based on lingering grievances imposed by each country, or by a shaky difference in morals. Coercion was largely thought to be at play. We were the country who suffered least from the repercussions and imposed the most—that is my belief, though history implies differently."

I pause abruptly at his words, wondering a bit at his interpretation. For it does imply a critique of Mathar, and that doesn't make sense to me. Though my allegiances are to Claralis above all, I do not know what to think of that, because I am loyal to Mathar secondly. I choose to brush it off, knowing that Halfern has good intentions, and whatever my qualms, there is value in his interpretation.

"You believe there'll be another war?" Dunet's eyes go wide, and her voice shakes.

"Only time will tell. While I feel conflict is painful, the hurts never heal. Whether one side is at fault and the other justified, history tends to favor Mathar and demonize those who stood against it. I feel that even I am too ignorant to the true cause of the war."

As Halfern talks, I find myself blinking at the area behind them. I scrunch my forehead, slipping away from the conversation. I try to concentrate again.

As much as I want to be with Dunet, I feel like I don't belong here.

But I try to focus on what he's saying again. Strangely, it occurs to me how familiar this feeling is.

Dunet looks at me at the end of the session, her eyes seeming to search my face anxiously, hands fidgeting, before she ducks them behind her back.

Still, I look at her with warmth and I hope my gentle expression shows. She has made much progress.

I can't help smiling every time she stumbles at an answer. Her growing curiosity at the world sends a warm ripple through my heartstrings.

I want to support her, no matter how I may feel about her decisions.

Is she making her own decisions, though? My influence on her has been so strong over the years, is it possible that ...?

I push back my shoulders, trying to reject that seed of doubt. Of course, she is acting on her own accord.

Halfern told me that she had taken a much greater interest in her lessons lately. It is a sobering thought to know that she is growing without me. It sends a shudder through me, knowing that every day that innocence I clung to will fade, but to deny it would only limit all that I know she can do. Past my own fears, I will always be proud of her.

I smile back at her affectionately.

She looks up at me in a way that tugs tenderly at my heart, even as it stings a little. "I'm glad you came, Sister."

"I hope that was all right."

"It was." She stares straight ahead at me, with a smile that twinges at its corners, but is so bright in every other way. "It was a little nerve-wracking ... But I think it helped me focus."

"You want me to come more often?" My heart rises a little. A part of it beats frantically, but I do long to be here with her.

She nods, her dimples creasing. "Yes!"

I take a breath and smile, gently pulling her into a hug and stroking at her hair. I feel every small line of the sister I know, and every quiver that I hadn't noticed before. How does she really feel?

"All right. If I have the time, I will." I bend down, kissing her forehead. I pull away, gazing at her for a moment. A calm smile settles over my features.

She smiles brightly in return, with just the barest hint of guardedness showing. Her smile manages to soothe me as much as it can at the moment, showing me that I'm hopefully doing the right thing. That is what I hope she's thinking. I'll come again if I can, but that shred of doubt presses at the back of my mind. I may not have much more time ...

When We Find Who We Are

Myllia

I stand there on the street, almost frozen in time.

A leaf caught in the middle of an unknown wind. And I'm at a crossroads.

I take a breath in.

My breathing feels faster all of a sudden, picking up to an almost unmanageable pace.

But I wanted to ask myself … who am I?

My mind wanders a little, as it always does, but something catches my eye. And it all seems to come to stillness.

I stop in the middle of the street, flows of people passing like ribbons and paying me no mind. I feel like I'm in my own world.

But there's a longing caught on my lips.

I tug on my dress. I'm still lost in my own dream, but what if I took a step?

A million possibilities swim in my mind, almost too frightening to answer.

But it's not fear that I feel. I feel caught up, as I clutch the collar of my lime green dress, hem of my skirt whirling beneath me.

Will I be a leaf forever, caught in the wind of my life?

I can't just live for Liela.

I can't just live for Dunet.

But they showed me who I am.

I take a step into the possibility before me.

Maybe I can heal? I want to bring people together, to know that my words can be used for good.

I'm told that I'm kind, and if that is who I am, then I want to give that kindness back to the world.

A tentative smile brushes my lips.

Clenine stands before me, its warm lights brushed by the cool chill of winter. It beckons me through the swirling flakes of fate.

It stands modest, but tall. Run down enough that it doesn't look expensive, but large enough to stand out on the street, and decorated enough with its fairly maintained lawn that it looks unique. It's a four-story building. That alone is uncommon. And though it's slightly drab, the flowers on the windowsills and the rising chimneys give it a homey feel. It's decorated along the path with brushes of silk and string, dyed stones and notes. And behind the windows, there's color and light.

Clenine

A School for All Ages & Abilities

Open to All

98

Dedicated to Andrea Cordre

I know what I will find.

They have a school of healing. Not just physical things, but people's feelings too.

Nieda had briefly mentioned it to me—that if she could, she would go.

Maybe I didn't understand it then ... or her, but maybe now I do a little.

I wonder what she would think of me now.

I miss her.

Not just because she was pretty, but because I thought of her as a childhood friend.

I wonder if she thought the same.

Maybe it's no time to wonder? I should do this. I can take this step.

And right now, it is for no one but myself.

I pull open the creaking wooden doors, etched with three squares per side and set with two eye-level windows. My heart lifts and I pull on the handles.

The opening room is musty, but neat. A few modest candle holders sit along the wall and the floor is of cool stone, set over with soft carpet of a mustard yellow.

A reception desk sits quietly, just inside the doorway, decorated lushly like a private office, a receptionist behind it.

"Hello!" The voice springs from a bubbly young woman in her mid-twenties with glasses, a soft face, bright eyes, and a relaxed smile. She stands up to address me and I see that she wears a dull yellow suit and knee-length skirt, and a scarlet headband in her dark-brunette hair. She sticks out her hand. "Name is Carlie!" She narrows her eyes, as she tilts her glasses. "Carlie Louise Onlett!" Then, she picks up her speech again. "Front end receptionist!"

I bring my hand up more delicately, meeting her eyes with a smile. "Myllia."

She looks questioningly at me, furrowing her brow at my dress. "How can I help you?"

I pull on my dress, for once looking around at everything and truly letting it all catch up with me. "I wanted to look at your program."

"Well then, sure thing!" Her smile seems to grow sunnier. "As you may know, we're a school for everyone. All ages. All incomes. From the generous donation of Lord Fenor Ren Cordre. That is the only reason we can keep this up. And his mother, Andrea Cordre, who gave us the funds to expand. Anyway." She shakes her head, smile still plastered on. "We have an assortment of programs—from the arts to science to the crafts to formalities." She waves her hand. "Endless, once you stop to think about it."

I tug at my bag. "I thought I heard that you had a healing program." Without realizing it, I'm a step closer to her.

"Yes, in fact, we do! Our medical program is quite robust compared to most anywhere this far north!"

I smile at her, feeling my own hope get ahead of me. "I meant ... Well, for people's feelings."

She shrugs at me. "Well, yes. Of course, we most definitely have that too! Fairly new, but it's shown a lot of interest, especially with the younger students. Would you like me to get you set up?"

"Yes, thank you."

She looks me up and down, "You ... won't be requiring any financial assistance, will you? Pardon me, but it's a required question. We get our less fortunate students paid for through donation."

"Oh, no ..." I stumble over my words a little. I know that I probably look out of place. "I think I'm fine."

"Wonderful!" She beams. "Shall we get started?"

"Yes, please."

She motions to the sparse, white cushioned, wooden chair. "Then, just a bit of paperwork."

I move over, resting in the chair, and crossing my ankles in front of me.

"Now." She leans forward. "Do you have any questions about the program? You're welcome to enroll in any standard and experimental courses alongside it."

"How does it work?"

"Well"—she taps a quill to the table—"I hear that it's very hands-on and experimental at this point. The jist of it is understanding yourself and your peers first, then the program moves on to more realistic and less structured sections with one of the older students or staff present, but I hear you do everything mostly on your own. They work through how to communicate sensitively, how to connect, and how to work through people's problems while not outright telling them what to do. It's about growth and guidance through what they already have." She shrugs again. "I'd tell you more, but like I said, it's a new program, and I'm not the most familiar with it. I was told it can get complicated."

"No need, but I would like to meet someone in charge of the program."

"Of course! Once you sign and pay, unless it would in any way help to meet first."

"No, I can wait." I scan over the paperwork, reading every word.

"Any questions?" She leans across the table.

"Not right now, but I would like to give everything some thought. I have a few last things I need to do. Can I bring this back?"

"Of course! But just so you know, we have a new group of students entering in three weeks. That would be the best time to enroll, if I do say so myself."

I bring my smile back up to her, gathering myself and rising. I correct my purse over my shoulder. "Thank you for all your time. I promise to be back."

She stands too, extending her hand again. "We look forward to your application! I've never heard of us turning anyone away, so let me just say that I'd be happy to welcome you!"

I take it. "And it was rather nice to meet you, Carlie."

Her smile brightens. "From all of us here, take care."

"You too."

I breeze out the door on light feet, then just let everything stand still and sink in at the top of the stairs. I can't help giggling, my knees springy, nearly jumpy, and I twirl, my eyes wet and stinging gratefully.

I stop and breathe in, giggling into my hand.

I did it!

For Liela. For Dunet.

But more importantly ... for me.

I stand up straight, the world bright.

I know that, even if my knees shake and my heart pounds, I can face my parents ...

Then I will sit and talk with Liela.

But whatever happens and whatever the world has in store for me ... I know I did this myself. For myself.

I close my eyes, my toes rising.

It feels like I've reached the sun, no matter that I can't see it.

The Hurts That Never Heal

Liela

"Liela." Myllia's voice touches me softly as she approaches.

I look up at her, my eyes moving to her beautiful, full figure, feeling some relief from the draining exhaustion that seems to cling to me daily. "What is it, Myllia?" I smile.

Her eyes take me in, and brush to my desk. "Are you all right?"

I let out a heavy sigh. "I suppose not." Then I brush it off for a weary smile.

She turns her cornflower eyes to me, her curls dancing in the candlelight, and she sinks as close as she can to me on the bed. "I know this is hard for you. You can tell me anything Liela."

I lean my head back and stretch, after so many hours of sitting at the desk. I move to sit next to her.

Myllia puts her hand to her mouth and giggles just slightly, before resting into my shoulder, placing her hand on the bed. I take it. She squeezes me, an inviting smile on her lips.

I start speaking in a low murmur, closing my eyes at her touch. "I can't stop thinking about her, Myllia. It makes me feel so broken."

She strokes my hand; the barest shiver runs up my spine. My mind feels so at ease, so settled in her presence. I feel like it's just us in the world, and I only concern myself with the words escaping my mouth. Everything slows down to the moment.

"I can't concentrate." It's true that every moment, awake or asleep, Dunet's pressing at my mind like a nightmare. And every time, I know that she could never be that. My thoughts keep circling, trapped, even as I try to keep moving forward like I always have. A shiver sets in my fingers and Myllia's grip seems to press on them harder, warming them up. "I keep imagining all those looks I missed—all that I missed about her."

"I know, Liela." She strokes my hair gently. Her kindness mends me. "But now, you understand that." Her voice grows certain. "You did know her, Liela."

I turn, even though I don't want to hide from Myllia, and I bite my lip. It stings. "Not well enough. I was blind ... And I should've been much better ..."

"Liela."

I look at her as she brings her pillowy arms around me.

"You did what you could. You always will do that for her ... I just know it."

I grasp her harder, my eyes building with haunting tears. I feel more unstable than I ever have before. I never thought I could feel this way.

Then, how must Dunet feel?

What do I have that she doesn't?

I wonder: Where did I stumble? When?

"It is okay to be afraid, Liela. I think she is too."

"She probably ..." I sit there for a minute, then feel my body shake as the truth comes out. "I know she is." But again, I am at a loss. What if I'm just ignoring her? I have to trust that I'm doing my best, though.

"You two are so brave and kind ... I know you will both get through this.

My grip tightens, and my voice comes out brittle. "Be there for her, Myllia ... If I can't."

I feel the barest tremor of her throat, but her voice is still so lovely against my ear. "I will be, Liela. Always."

I regret saying it. It slashes my heart, even if a weight leaves it with the comfort she offers. But I know I can't always be there. "What do you think is going through her mind, Myllia?" My voice is heavy.

"Liela, I can't answer that for her. I think you understand."

"I do, Myllia ... that's what scares me. I just wonder if she's leaving things out to protect me. That should be"—my hand grips tighter to her— "that should be something for me to take up. Not her."

Through everything, Myllia is still there, clutching me like I'm all that matters. "It is because she's like you, Liela."

I remain in the silence that I leave after her words, letting them burn a little, because she's right.

She stirs against me, reaching for my cheek, and pulls back a little, her words steady and firm and soft. "And that is all right."

I nod, feeling almost like a lost child in a commander's shoes. "Thank you, Myllia. Myllia?" I meet her eyes. "Are you all right?"

"Yes, Liela." I can hear that reassuring touch in her voice. "I am sorting out a few things for myself. It is because of you and Dunet. I want to tell you all about it, but this is something I have to do on my own."

I look back at her with raised eyebrows as a strange uncertainty stirs inside me. I want to know, so I can be there for her like she is for me.

"You should not worry, Liela. It is something that seems so simple now. After that, I can move on ... And I will discuss my future with you." Her face lightens.

I stare at her, blinking for a moment. My heartbeat flutters a little.

"You are gawking, Liela," Myllia teases with a twinkle in her eyes.

"You always have more confidence than you let on, Myllia. I think you know what you want more than anyone."

"I never used that confidence until you came into my life. You brought it out, Liela." She shifts her eyes so delicately and mine collapse at their gentleness, my cheeks alive with my pounding heart. She tucks into me again, and I feel comforted against her lush form. "We all have that strength; we just need to use it. Will you be all right now?"

I inhale, with a small smile. "Yes, Myllia. You always cheer me up somehow."

She pulls away and whispers, "Liela?"

I blink at her, and she pulls forward a little, her eyes teasing.

Oh. That's what she wants.

I smile and nod. We pull into a tender kiss. I let myself bathe in this moment and the warmth and kindness she brings.

She lets go, giggling and then turns all the prettiness of her cornflower eyes to me. "I am always here, Liela. I will let you be there for me soon, but I need to know I can do this for myself first. I am scared, Liela, but more so ... I am thrilled, because I know I can do this, and I want to find the confidence in myself." Her smile turns radiant, and she whispers, "Then I want to share that part of me with you ..." She trails off and I let myself be caught up in her new dream—whatever it is—before it even starts.

I have trouble letting go of that need to cling for her answer, but I feel that same thrill for her as my heart stumbles. Maybe the only girl I knew was the one that loved me? But she is so much more than that. She always was and I always knew that, deep in my heart. So, I know, whatever is best for her is what I want for her.

And now I can't stop laughing, as I fall into her cushy arms and feel the gentle daze of her against me.

Even if I want her to stay, she pulls away again, pecking at my cheek and getting up out of bed. "Good night, Liela."

I hold her there for as long as possible.

The Resolve to Find Your Way

Myllia

My mind drifts as I gaze longingly out the carriage window, releasing a heavy sigh. I fold my hands over my lap, the definition of calm, or at least as calm as I can make them, so that I don't fiddle with my dress on the ride. My thoughts are settled on the future, but no longer in a daydream.

I breathe in to try to settle my racing heart. Today, I will stand up for myself. I know exactly what I want, and I hold my hand against my heart, trying to feel that certainty that I can believe in. Liela made me realize that I can. She made me see who I am.

I find it hard not to envy the bond Liela and Dunet share. I know that, no matter what, they will be all right. And I will have something completely different. I mean something different to each of them. Something completely my own.

Though they will be all right, I find it hard not to be scared for them. I want to be there, regardless. Dunet made me realize what my own choices could mean—that I do not just have to wait. Wait for whatever will happen to me to catch up. Wait to be my own person ... After all, I know what I want. Liela accepted it. She chose me, like I chose her.

They all deserve the best me. I want Liela to have that. Dunet needs that too.

Maybe I do not have everything thought through, but I do know that I cannot be aimless forever.

You can do so much with your kindness, Myllia. It feels like such a long time ago. I shrugged it off like it meant nothing. But it does mean something. I let it sit in my heart for all this time, thinking of the possibility that I can be so much more.

Maybe I'll stop daydreaming? I can live for both Liela and myself, and I will take the reins of my future.

That starts with asserting my happiness—what I know will make me *more* than content.

I know perfectly well what I have and who I am. I just need to do something with that knowledge.

Both Liela and Dunet faced their fears and now it's time for me to face mine.

I let out another breath as the carriage comes to a stop. My gaze lingers on the frost covered plains and neatly cropped hedges set into the side of the sprawling manor. A splendid place, really. A place that I dreamed in, and wasted away. I let myself dream. I really think it is something that everyone does. How different am I really from Dunet, or even Liela?

I steady myself on the carriage railing, finding my footing on the grounds of the estate.

I never even realized I was lonely; that there was a gap in my heart that I could only fill with fairytales, people and places in the sheltered whimsy of dreams.

I thought I was content to just dream, until I found the dream I sought and realized that it was just the beginning for me.

I move over the grounds, my head clearer and refinement set in elegant purpose. More than in the past, for I know that I'm a different girl now, and my eyes can't be clouded for this.

For a moment, I try to mimic Liela's confidence, but it's clearly not mine and I raise a hand to giggle. My confidence looks different—not as pronounced—and that's okay.

For a moment, my eyes linger on the fountains and the beautifully inlaid windows. I can't see it as ugly. No, it is just part of my past, like any other place. I was far from depressed—only content.

I move past the perfectly trimmed hedges and flower beds, fountains gurgling past the hedges' corners. Spans of lawns open up nearer to the estate.

Before I can stop to think, the sprawling double doors are ahead of me, chiseled ivory on marble columns. For the first time, I swallow, my hands coming back down to the fringes of my dress. I would go with my fate, if this were happening earlier, but I know I just can't now ... Not any longer.

My hand does not shake, but reaches for the door with a clarity in a future I would build for myself. Not what will be given to me, but something that only I can do.

Iren pulls open the door to the estate with aging fingers and my heart stills. Even if I was distant from them, I would rather see any of my family's servants before I meet my parents. Iren stands straight in his bony frame, with his pointed nose, and thin, resolute posture. The hallway sits wide and dim behind him—shaded mahogany and polished beams across the arched ceiling. The entryway looks more like a reception area than anything, with a desk, and a silver and crimson-stained chandelier. The living room seems to glow delicately from the left, and the dining area shines too, to the right.

"Lady Laundra." He bows courteously. "It is a pleasure to welcome you home."

I pull on a kind smile, although my skin feels paper thin. "Iren. It is nice to see you too."

"Will you be staying long? I will have your room prepared."

I look straight at him, my smile small, but purposeful. "I would appreciate it if I could see my parents, thank you. I appreciate it though."

He bows to me again and I sigh under my breath. "Your parents are unavailable at the moment."

Of course, I knew they would be. I find myself reaching for the crease of my cuff again, as my moment of resolve stretches out. "You can tell them that I am waiting, then."

"Of course," Iren says with a dip of his head. "Let me prepare some tea." He starts backing away, raising himself.

"Iren ..."

"Yes?"

"I really have no need for pleasantries. If you insist, though, I will be grateful." I pull on another smile to express as much of my gratitude as I can muster.

Iren leads me through an arch into the west wing and I follow his crisp lead, my eyes trapped by this not-so-distant memory that seems twisted and of an eternal slumber—something I was unaware of at the time.

"I will let them know you're here. Please, make yourself comfortable, Lady Laundra."

He leaves.

I gaze over the living room—the spotless, evenly spaced furniture, cushioned and inlaid with soft stones and pale-ornate chandeliers dangling from the polished beams of the ceiling. I move to a red velvet armchair near the window, staring out at the frosted fields and the distant forests and mountains on the northern horizon. I used to read in this room. Stories of kindness and hardship. I loved happy endings the most, and I loved romance more than anything. I always dreamed of those stories, passively imagining myself in one of those endings, until I had the will to carve my own—to expect more from myself. I'm so close to the ending I want ... That ending is only my beginning to something much richer.

So much led me to Liela. She was the person I needed to complete myself, and now I'm ready to be everything I know I can be.

Iren enters once more, carrying a teacup. He brings it over to me, setting it on the table to my right. I never seemed to notice how wrinkled his fingers were, and they make me wonder if maybe he is too old for his job. I wonder if I will see Nieda. I resist my sigh. She was my maid for several years, but she was the closest thing I had to growing up with someone. I let out a breath. I had a crush on her too, one that could have led to something, even though I think she did have an interest in men ...

I take the cup, sinking back into the red velvet chair to take a sip. "Thank you, Iren."

"Of course, Lady Laundra." He dips his head and steps away from me, leaving me alone in the room once again.

I give a tight sigh, sinking back into the cushions, and I turn my head out the window again. Part of me wishes I brought Liela with me, but I know I need to do this alone. This is my fate I am grasping at. It feels right for me to face this on my own. When it is all done, I will talk to her about our future.

I find myself nearly drifting into aimless thought as Iren enters the room again after a time. "Your parents will see you at seven this evening. I apologize, Lady Laundra."

I feel a sinking in to my stomach, whether I was ready or not. I don't know whether to sit tight or let that all dissipate. "Thank you, Iren. You have done more than enough. I will be heading up to my rooms."

He takes his leave once more, etching another bow, and I pull myself up from my seat, looking back at the living room again as I leave. Then, moving through the polished hall, echoes murmur off the sturdy wood and intricate, expensive rugs.

I ascend the wide, carpeted stairway up to the second story landing, finding myself in my room—just how it was when I last saw it. A neat room—my plush, yellow armchair by the window, shelves of books along the adjoining wall, and a clean-sheeted, curtained bed on the opposite wall.

Yes, all is neat except a corner stacked with pillows and strewn with books, ribbons, and lace, curtained in pastels of pink, purple, orange, yellow, red, and white, with a carpet underneath, and set with dozens of unlit candles. It's a room adorned in fairytale light and the magic of imagination. Close and warm. This was my cradle. This small pocket of fantasy and the gardens I walked though, imagining so many fantasy endings, so many chance occurrences. But this room and the gardens outside are no longer my future. Solitude is not what I seek.

I pick up a small hair clip, adorned with a lavender bow. I hold it gently to my breast. I still love the girl I was, but I also admire the woman I am becoming. She was not much different, really …

I look up at the timepiece on my wall, its hands at seven.

Taking one last breath to collect myself, I gather all of my confidence.

I make my way down the wide, carpeted stairs. My parents' house always smelled floral—lavender, especially. I breathe it in. It's a pleasant scent that I always liked. Our estate is known for its gardens, and they are well-kept, though by the estate's servants and not my parents.

I find myself in the east wing dining room, met by tall windows, dangling chandeliers, and ornate display pieces on the antique furnishings that surround the lengthy, polished dining table.

My parents are already seated there, complemented by the table's old-fashioned elegance. I move to sit across from them.

I sit properly—a mirror of grace. I run my fingers over the moonlit-violet-embroidered arm of my chair, thinking about what I have to say. My mind runs though all my options as I try to keep it as level as it can be.

I look up to meet the placid indifference of my parents. They were absent, neglectful. Not harsh or commanding. Not clearly abusive in any way. Not cruel. Just … not there for me. They were always absent from my life, and that was it. No emotional support or care or outward signs of love. I found those things in books. They expected me to be married as a lady and that was all. I expected nothing from them. But I will ask them for something today: to respect my choices and recognize who I am not—who I am and who I know I can be.

"What did you come here for, Myllia?" It is the dismissive voice of my mother.

I bring myself up straighter, hands kept on my lap. "I want to talk to you about my future."

Father stiffens, his face darkening for once.

"I ask that you cancel my marriage and that I be enrolled in Clenine." Clenine, Claralis' place of learning, with people from all walks of life. No tutors, no confinement to people of my station.

"That is unacceptable, Myllia," comes father's constructed voice.

I breathe in, collecting myself. "Father. Mother. I just want to tell you that I have a goal now. I want to move forward with my life. I do not expect you to accept that, but I expect you to allow it."

"Myllia, you know we put a lot of work into this marriage," Mother says with a tinge of scorn and an edge to her words.

"I understand that, but I have someone."

"Who is it?" asks father sternly, his eyes narrowing and nearly dangerous, something I have never seen.

I have always been just right in the respects that mattered. I never protested my fate for the small hopes I harbored. I wanted to make them happy, at least. I hesitate. I almost tell them who Liela is—that I am marrying the Commander. But I will not use Liela for that. This is my battle—it is a matter of principle.

Even so, my reluctance to mention her may be because I'm a little scared of what they will think of ... her.

I take a controlled breath in, smiling at my resolve. I can't do that—I know that. I will trust in myself. "It is someone I love, and I will marry her of my own accord and my own choice. It is not my place to tell you who she is. Mom ... Dad ... I am calling off the arranged marriage and I will enroll in Clenine." My thoughts feel so rapid at this point, that I can barely keep track of them. "I want you to understand that this is my decision." I say it more forcefully, more at ease, although my heart is racing. My resolve is the clearest it has ever been, and I can hear that clarity in my calm voice. "I want to study to help people. I want to heal peoples' pain and understand them. And, I want to walk that path with the person I love."

They sit there frozen, aghast, and taken aback. For a moment, I shake in my chair, not knowing what will come. But I settle myself: I will take their response, however it is, and still push forward.

"Myllia—" I hear my father's building disbelief and see the shock written on my mother's face.

"I do not ask for your agreement, but I ask for your approval. As parents, I want you to know that I have a path set for myself."

My dad's fingers tap on the table, his jaw set dangerously.

"We never expected this from you, Myllia," comes the disbelieving voice of my mom.

"I never expected it from myself either, but I want to strive for more than what you gave me. I want to use what I have. I do not expect you to understand, but I promised myself this. I expect better from myself, and I want you to want that for me too."

My dad narrows his eyes, forehead wrinkled. "She?"

My heart drops ever-slightly, but I stand up tall and say it with all my strength. "Yes."

Mother looks at me, on the verge of a breath. "Myllia"—her mouth is tight— "you have my consent, if not my approval." I feel a surge of shock and a small, unexpected bloom of hope stir at my hear. Maybe she saw something in me? Just maybe.

My head spirals, but I can't quite feel grateful.

Dad looks at me directly, eyes hard, but not completely closed off. "I will put off the marriage and consult with your mother. Let me just say that I am disappointed, but also surprised. I didn't expect this from you, Myllia. You have my consent ... And I reluctantly admit my respect."

I keep the shock from my face, as my chest trembles. While things could still end badly with my parents, I want to thank them for what they have seen in me and the small hope their answers give me in moving forward. "Thank you," I say with sincere gratitude, pushing away the lingering cold.

I do not know what the future holds, but even so, I have made a start to it.

"I will use my future in the best way that I can find. And ... Her name is Liela ..." I say with a soft smile, her name brushing off my lips like a warm future, a home ... And the person who convinced me that this moment was possible.

I turn, letting myself imagine what I want their faces to show, and not expecting to return anytime soon—I will put this place behind me, but I will always acknowledge who I was. I have tested my fears and am now fully ready to walk my own path.

"No matter how I feel about you both, you will be welcome at my wedding, and you can be part of my future." A small invitation, welcoming them to create a new relationship with me. The rest is up to me, but I refuse to be a bitter person. I hope to someday see the best in them. Their response shook me, but it also showed me that there was some understanding and care under their indifference. Maybe they didn't know any better—how to show love. And

I want to be a better person to show them that they can be too.

As I leave, I finally realize how much I'm shaking ...

But it's okay, because no matter what happens, I am walking my own future.

Caroline Sophia Hamel

A Heart Gone Cold

Driena

I thought I was just right.

That I was good in everyone's eyes.

That I was the role model my sister needed.

The perfect, starry daughter my parents wanted.

I thought I was everything ... When I was nothing.

Only now am I someone worthy to have love, faith, and dreams put into her.

I was a weak girl and a fragile girl. So, I threw her away. I didn't need her anyway.

It never mattered. Because no one misses her ...

The world is better off now that I killed the girl in my shadow—the girl who was me and didn't know any better.

Maybe I killed my childhood, but that is fine with me. It is better for everyone.

I wasn't practical or smart. I wasn't special. I had no right to carry anything or hold anything in my small hands. The world went through her head.

I deserved that naïve world to fall apart underneath my carefree feet and self-contained mind.

That light had only given me fragile dreams that lasted only so long. Those dreams will never come back, but what I found in its place is far more stable.

I don't want to throw away Liela's dreams, but they seem far too familiar.

That makes me scared for her.

My sister looked up to me. I was her everything and I failed her.

I ... I'm still fragile. I still cry alone. More than I thought was possible. Maybe I looked away, so that I felt like I could find something in Liela.

Because she called to me at my lowest.

Maybe I just found her optimism so tempting and I wanted to contain it and hold it in a bottle. She drives me, but more than that, maybe I see who I could've been ...

She really is a like-minded soul. She's my star-soul, my sister, more than my actual one, and I wouldn't have it any other way.

As awful as that sounds, my sister deserves and always did deserve a far better person to call her sister.

Caroline Sophia Hamel

Falling Apart

Dunet

I think I knew that I was falling apart for a while.

I acknowledge everyone.

I smile.

I give the joyful-sounding reply that is expected of me.

But I've never felt so alone.

So cold.

I hate it.

I hate this world that I've made for myself—a knotted cage that I let strangle me.

But to come out of it … looks so much colder.

I want to embrace the cold. I have always known that what I need to bring to everyone is a smile. Anything else would be a burden.

I'm selfish for locking myself up, but I feel like it would be worse otherwise.

Every choice I make I hate.

It stabs at me. My heart is cold. My eyes are cold.

And I have an ever-present desire for something sharp.

It makes no sense. I was always perfectly carefree and fine in everyone's eyes. Yet, everything grew to be so suffocating.

I'm falling too fast.

What's happening to me?

Do I really care anymore?

But I do.

I think I want Liela to come save me. Or Myllia.

Maybe Myllia?

Because more than anything, it's suffocating to even think about telling Liela. It makes me want to scream. To claw my eyes out.

And I would. If there would be no one to hear me or see me after … But there is.

Is it selfish to talk to Myllia?

What does that make me?

The First Breath

Liela

I roll my eyes as Darnor saunters over to me across the thin span of the battlements, but I take a bow anyway, arms sweeping outward and eyes turned upward. "Lord Darnor Veln!" A given display from me at this point. I could tease him with the title all day. It just rolls off the tongue far more than he deserves.

I honestly don't know why we meet here. I think it's a habit. It feels like a nice perch to the world, and it became our little meeting point.

He laughs, demeanor growing more casual. "Liela! I heard you wanted to see me."

"Yes, I miss you. You know, while I see you almost more than my family now, it's still less than old times. I even spend more time with Driena now."

"And I thought you wouldn't have time for me!"

"I still have a little." I lean my elbows over the wall, gazing at the fields and distant forests in Siltheus' direction. A sigh escapes me. "I wonder if they'll come, Darnor."

He glances at me and joins me against the wall. "You know, I feel sorry for you."

"I appreciate the sentiment. I'm exhausted!"

"I could never do it, you know." He slumps his shoulders.

I chuckle. "Oh, I know." I sit there for a moment, collecting my breath. "Darnor?"

He glances over at me, eyes light, open, and kind—how I've always known them to be. It puts my heart at ease, just how easy he is to talk to. Driena is a different story—a much more complicated one. I grimace internally. She's like a sister, but it's like I sometimes have to push my words out to her. And then I have to face a judgement I never have to with Darnor.

I close my eyes. "I want to tell you something." I open them again, the sky a pool of brilliant stars, endless and welcoming.

"About Myllia?"

I turn to him with raised eyebrows; my face heats up. "How did you know?"

"I think it's obvious to the people who know you." He stares off. "Maybe it should be harder to see, but I know you, Liela. It makes me happy to see you like that."

I close my eyes, a warm feeling in my heart. "Thank you, Darnor," I whisper.

"Always ..." His smile is gentle and the corners of mine lift at it. He eases into a grin. "Care telling me how you met?"

I roll my eyes. "I would never dream of it. Rather ..." I breathe in, eyes closing again.

"You don't have to, Liela."

I smile at him with a laugh. "If there's anyone that I want to tell first, I want it to be you. Trust me, it makes everything easier."

"Then Driena?"

I shrug, sighing. "For now, I think so. But right now, I haven't even told my parents."

He nods. "Take your time."

I turn back to the stars, eyes focused, but far off. "It was in a courtyard. She was beautiful, Darnor ... I can never describe it. Of course, I was awfully dense ..."

"Of course." He chuckles. "As you are. But I think you knew then."

I breathe in, my eyes closed. "I did. I always did. And I don't know at what point she knew it was something more ... It was always her who knew herself better. I admire and love that about her. I realized it when we danced, and everything connected—before she put it into words. Everything seems to slow down with her. Maybe nothing is perfect, but with her, I feel like everything stops ..."

"It sounds pleasant."

I shake my head. "More than I can ever say."

He lets out a breath. "You know, I'm glad you turned me down, because you have this. Not that you could've done anything else. I know that now."

I shake my head. "Are you getting sentimental now, of all times?" I laugh out loud into the night.

He laughs back, good-naturedly. "Apparently, I am!" He softens again. "Thank you, Liela, for trusting me. When it gets time to tell Driena, or your family, or the world, I'll be there."

My eyes feel a little glassy. "I don't think there's any need for that much drama." But it settles deep in my heart. "Thank you, Darnor."

"If I could do anything, then I would. Liela, you're my best friend. I wanted to tell you that at least once."

I close my eyes against the cold wind, somehow so comforting in a world that is so volatile. "So much still scares me, Darnor, but this is something I stopped being scared of." I turn back to him. "Thank you for being such a good friend." I connect eyes with him, that understanding falling between us. It's a trust without expectation that I think I can only find in his friendship.

A Playfulness Long Gone

Dunet

I swing my legs out below me, numbly.

Torie watches me with a frown, then smiles warmly. "You've been awfully quiet, Dunet." Her brow creases.

I tug on a smile. "Oh …" I shake my head.

She bends her knees a little, placing her hands over them, and gets down to eye-level. "I'm worried about you."

I giggle unconvincingly. "I'm all right!"

"Okay." She shakes her head. "But you wanted to help me with this, right?"

"Right!" I beam, even though it feels hollow.

"I'm going to graduate soon and move up, so I won't have much time anymore." Her eyes turn down just a little, then they meet mine. "I really am sorry, but I know Kreenie and Lunan will be happy to have you."

I nod quickly as I swallow hard, my mind drifting away from her already, wanting her to move on. I barely see her. The room. Almost like she no longer exists to me. Almost like I left this place, because it's leaving me anyway. Torie and the others will all go.

"Can you peel these?" She hands me some potatoes.

"Yes!" I sputter.

She looks sidelong at me with a smile. Her look is ... clouded.

I try not to tune out. Try not to let everything blur past me. I beam back at her, my eyes broken behind their spark. If anyone would notice in the kitchens, it would be her. Yet, I don't know if I want her to.

Kreenie bounds up a moment later, pigtails spinning—her bright yellows and pinks set off a smile I can't help, the plaid of her skirt and suit standing out, her thick form bouncing to her every step, seeming carefree. "Dunet! What are you peeling?" She looks over my shoulder.

I hold it out to her. "Some potatoes!"

"Oh!" She pulls at her pigtails, then takes my hands. "Want to come with me?"

Torie gives her a look, then turns away, going back to her cutting.

I swallow. I would rather stay with Torie. Maybe she is more perceptive, but at least I never have to overdo pretending to have fun. Kreenie is fun, but she's been off-putting to me lately. She seems bubbly all the time. I wonder how she does it? Sometimes I wish I could too. "Sure, Kreenie!"

Torie grabs the potato and peeler from my hands and nudges me. "Have fun with her!" Her eyes linger on me too long, even though her smile remains encouraging.

"I will!" I spark. I don't want to leave Torie. My throat aches already. She's leaving me already. Leaving me alone. And now, I just want to push her away and let it be over.

I know she doesn't mean it.

But like everyone … she's leaving me behind.

I can't go where she's going.

My eyes prick with empty tears, before they disappear, like they never existed, and I'm left dry.

I want to throw Torie away, but I also want to clutch her, to hold her.

It feels like everyone's leaving me, tossing me out while thinking that I'm okay.

I'm not. I never was.

Kreenie takes my hand and pulls me in a flurry. I want to smile, like I haven't a care in the world, but I can't. I just feel a cold shiver.

It doesn't matter.

She giggles and spins me, and I join her in a skip. I wear the white ribbon I always do now, set over my buttery, tucked-back hair like a headband. My hair cascades in waves down my back, a little less messy now. It's the ribbon that I got from them and that I wear for my sister—wear it for purity—for the fantasy I want to let everyone else live. "I want to show you something, Dunet!"

I want to say I hate her. She's so tone deaf, so cheerful …

But I know the real answer is that I hate myself …

She doesn't deserve it. She's wonderful.

I wish I could be like her.

I'm empty. Absent.

And no one sees that.

In the moment, I wish I could just reach for one of the knives set aside in the kitchen, to silence these thoughts and myself. To free everyone from my burden.

How could they love me? How could anyone love me?

And like every second of every day, I wish that I was alone.

At the same time, I want to reach out.

I know that I'm a horrible contradiction that just wants to hurt. I can't have it both ways. Because I want everything.

Yet, I want nothing.

I want everything to go.

I wonder if they're acting on my behalf.

They must be.

Maybe just like I am.

Except that I know I'm worse. Because for me, everyone is selfless for some reason. It stabs at my cold heart.

I want to peel myself away from this world.

I even stopped caring how they looked at me … Or at least, I tell myself that I don't care. But like always, I'm still acting.

For a reason I can't name.

A Familiar Difference

Torie

Kreenie bounces in her seat next to me. I don't even think she notices.

She looks curiously at me as I measure ingredients.

"What's that?"

"I'm measuring the cinnamon for the apple spice cake. We measure it with—"

"That looks just like"—she interjects—"Like how you measured that soup thing!" She beams, looking proud of herself.

"Yes, Kreenie; it is." I try to be patient with her. Sometimes I do enjoy her well-intentioned obliviousness.

"But, I forgot what it's called. It looks so delicious though!" She reaches for it without thinking.

I roll my eyes and let her take it, as she rolls the dough in her fingers and studies it intently, without seeming bored in the slightest, even if she's off-task—still bouncing in her seat.

"You know, you're a great cook, Torie, and you're pretty!" Her words start to flow over each other, as she jumps from one subject to another. "You know, the other day I was thinking—"

I smile inwardly at Kreenie's disruption and her tangent that isn't self-aware. I've gotten used to her eccentricities by now. It's just her way of communicating. If people listened to her, they'd see that she has a lot of great ideas, and her childlike heart is golden.

For my part, I try to affirm her. I've had my share of bullying, and I don't want Kreenie to be part of that. I ... feel a bit ashamed that I initially tried to admonish her so much. If anything, she's really good at what she does, with the right support.

"—And I told Thomas that we should cook the fish like this, and he agreed with me! He said he'd think about it! Isn't that great?" She flicks at her pigtail a few times and smiles at the ceiling.

"It's great, Kreenie!" I meant it.

"I know! It made me so happy! I thought I'd tell you and see what you thought." She nods to herself.

We finish our task as the lunch break comes around, and she bounds off five minutes early without explanation, her arms flapping a little at her sides. She hums a cheerful tune to herself that I recognize by now.

I sigh after she leaves. I was always the odd one out, anyway. I should've understood her sooner. She's different, and that's okay. I guess it just took me a while to realize that.

A Hearth of Warmth

~ Memory ~

Liela

Do the things we love ever truly leave us?

As much as I want to curl my fists around mother and send a retort, I always remember the softness that she used to have for me.

I remember it so sweetly, sweeping me up in these confusing tides of memory.

I want that back. I could never admit it to her, but I do.

"My dear." She touches her palms against my cheeks. "I love you. Your father and I will be proud of whatever you do. Whoever you'll be."

She rises up, her image a splendor of poise and elegance. My eyes sparkle at her image. Did I forget that? That I wanted to be like her, just as much as Father?

She took me riding. It was a normal day, and it was the last memory of her smile that I can remember.

"Liela," comes her soft voice that I cling to.

"When you love someone, you give them everything. Did you know that?"

"No." I shake my head, staring over the field of daisies.

"My mother gave me all her love. I received her gift of the court. Your father gave me laughter. My sister gave me the world. You know what I did with that?"

I furrow my brow.

"I lived a good life for her."

"Mother?"

"I know you never knew her." She pecks me on the cheek.

I cast my eyes back at the flowers. I find my tongue tight. I never did. I feel like I should say something, but it all eludes me.

Her eyes turn muddled. "I wish you did. Your grandmother on your father's side loves flowers. You know, she was there for me when no one else was? I was happy to take the Cordre name. That was the only time I was so scared that I didn't know what to do." Her arms rest across my chest. "I would tell you not to grow up, but that's life and I know you're strong. And you're mine. Remember that." Her smile turns far off. "You're just like your father." While it settles nicely, something about how she says that feels off, even though I love father and look up to him, and I squirm in the saddle. Mother never notices, so I press back into her touch as she grasps the reigns.

I started looking to the distance between me and her and the closeness of her and Dunet ...

I rest with my eyes, feeling the warmth of the room, like I'm inside a bottle of light. I lean against father's shoulder on the couch, my hair tied back. Pronounced, but laid-back.

The warmth of the fire tickles at my cheeks. The small stars cascade in a twinkling canvas across the floor-to-ceiling windows. The room is like a dream—something warm and soft.

Mother sits in a rocking chair, stoic-looking and elegant, holding Dunet on her lap. I turn my eyes to them, hands wringing against my trousers. Mother gives me a soft smile, before looking back to Dunet with bright eyes.

I can hear the timbre in father's voice as he hums softly, and I awkwardly try to hum along.

He sends a humorous smile down at me that makes me wiggle my toes.

Then he ruffles my hair, laughing heartily, and I break out into a laugh and a broad grin with him.

I look up to that face I admire and adore. He's my father and my role model. Him and mother are the most competent, hard-working, and kind people I know. I want to model them both.

"What are you humming, darling?" Mother asks, her eyes kind, while Dunet's tiny ones shine on us. I always felt

that they were the purest, most beautiful color blue I'd ever seen. Sapphire. They were from the moment she came into my life. I knew I loved her then.

"Song of the River Angel."

Mother gives a doting smile and turns to Dunet. "Would you like to hear, sweetie?"

Dunet stares up at her with wide, sparkling eyes, her form enraptured.

"How about you my wren?"

I look up with a matching spark to Dunet's eyes, yet nowhere near her brightness. "I would like to hear it."

Mother smiles affectionately at the two of us, readjusting Dunet gently on her lap. "This is the song from the night your father and I first met. He was ... quite the fool."

I snicker under my raised hand and father winks.

Mother takes a breath.

She is a beauty

In a world of love

A lady of the river

Sings a hymn of love

To her darling prince

Away on stary seas

It calls to him through time

To draw his heart to ease

A prince to cherish

With a heart of love

And a wealth of kindness

Burdens left on wings of doves

And so,

Her darling prince comes

His brow only starlight

And his offer a wish to her heart

A prince beyond the brush of air

The caress of heat

A prince in heart

And not in deeds

Heart above desire

Caroline Sophia Hamel

Soul above lust

On wings of purity

They find each other in a rain of dust

I thought I remembered her brushing my hair and crying.

"Where did my child go?"

Though, maybe it was something else. Could that really have been my mother?

I let them all be fractured memories...

How much did I love her? Was there really a world where there wasn't a coldness between us?

Maybe I'm wrong, but it all started when I was a teenager.

All of a sudden, it was either distance or arguing.

Does that make it my fault, or did she really never love me? I thought she did.

Mother frowns at my regalia, parading after Father.

"Fenor. What do you think you're doing?"

"I like it, Mother. I'm a proud knight." I lift my head.

She pulls Father aside. I know I shouldn't, but I go to listen. "It's going to her head. You know I respect you, but the military? She needs to learn some decency first. She's far too impulsive and she's acting up. She's sensitive when she doesn't get her way."

"Fern." Father's voice is commanding and soothing at the same time. I feel at ease, even if I shiver a little at the fear of an argument over me.

I peek around the corner, catching him pull my mother's hand to his lips as if to console her.

"You worry too much. I think she makes a fine knight."

"Have you heard her? She's spouting such nonsense ideals and turning them into arguments against me. When I tell her not to, she cries." She shakes her head in disappointment. "It's infuriating. She needs to grow a spine and some respect."

"She's a teenager, Fern."

"Since when did you take all her attention? She hates me now." Her voice spikes in irritation. "She takes every chance to snap at me."

"Fern, be easy on her. She's finding her way. She just thinks you're attacking her. She doesn't see it like you do."

"Nonsense." She draws her hand back abruptly from Father. "She always has this theatrical justification for the tiniest things. It's like she's trying to make me mad."

"It's her way of doing things. She tries, Fern."

"She doesn't do it right, though. If only she would just do what I tell her to do. She's lazy, Fenor. It's 'I'll be a knight this' or 'I'll be a knight that,' but when I try getting her to do anything else she won't listen. When she can't be a knight, she's just lazy. I can't get her to do her practical studies. It's like she won't listen to anything or conveniently forgets unless it matters to her. I'm just sick and tired of her willful misbehavior."

"I know it feels that way, Fern. I see how hard you try." Father starts leading Mother away to their room as they continue to talk about me. I feel a strong hope that Father continues to defend me.

I duck away from the opening, my heartbeat frantic.

I feel a bit distant from my own head, before anger rises in me. I don't think I did anything wrong, did I?

I pull my knees into my grasp, trying to think but coming up blank.

I'm a knight! I'll save my people.

I smile.

But I don't really get what she said.

I do everything exactly how I should. I try hard at everything. Father praises me for that.

Why is she mad at me?

There always seems to be something preventing me from doing something she asks in the exact way she expects me to do it. Somehow, I mess up every time.

I do it wrong.

I take too long.

I ask her too many questions or have her repeat herself.

I forget.

Or someone tells me to do something else. It takes me forever then, which only makes sense.

How does me explaining myself to her count as me arguing? It's only fair that I can. I feel a little tense.

I'll get better. I'll make her proud, so we don't have to argue. Won't that make her proud too? It's not enough for me to just have Father or my new sister.

I'll show everyone that I can be a fine knight, protect everyone, and I'll make my parents proud. She'll see.

I raise my head, feeling a bunch of new energy. I'll drive myself forward, protect my new sister, and do everything that I can to be the perfect leader.

Mother will have to see me for what I am if I do that—that I'm trying.

I feel an unrestrained smile. My reasoning sounds perfect in my ears. After all, what's wrong with being an idealistic knight? I've always dreamed of that.

Something That Wants to Give

Liela

I come and join Darnor against the barrack wall, fence-line of the practice rings not too distant. Letting myself slide down to a seated position, I'm hidden enough that no one really notices me.

Darnor is watching her with soft eyes, as her harsh eyes take in every move of the trainees, before her feedback comes out matter-of-fact.

"She's difficult, isn't she?" I lean back, looking at the sky.

He laughs. "Of course, she is! That's why I love her, though. Why we both do."

I raise my eyebrows and turn to him. "So, you do?"

"It was never a secret. At least, not to me. Not anymore."

I shake my head, looking back at her.

"She's even more stubborn about these things than you are," he says. "I might just outright tell her soon."

My eyes gleam. "You should. You know, Darnor, I don't think you know this, but it would mean the world to me. You're my two best friends. I couldn't imagine anything better."

He chuckles. "You know, I think I will." Then he grins. "If only to see her face, that is."

"Oh, she'll deny it!" I laugh.

"Highly likely!" His face turns serious. "So, what is a Commander doing with a lowly Lord and questionable student?"

"Oh ..." I sigh. "Just relieving myself of insurmountable pressure and dread. It's nice from time-to-time." I crack a strained grin.

"If you say so." His eyes soften. "Are you okay, Liela?"

"With the world likely ending, probably not." I shrug.

"Which topic are you talking about?"

"Both, really. Every day is another day less to prepare for what's coming. But Dunet feels worse, and I use Myllia to forget it all. Now, I would say, well ..." I put my hand over my forehead, lean back, and groan. "Sometimes, I don't want to be Commander."

He looks forward, his eyes considerate. "I could see that."

"If I fail—"

"You won't." He turns to me with a comforting smile.

"But ..." I clench my fingers.

"You have us."

I laugh heartily. "Easy for you to say!"

"Liela, you are never alone in this. I could see it feeling like that."

"I know. But sometimes it feels like I'm holding up the world."

"Which, I think I can safely say, no one can handle alone."

I sigh. "I wish I could."

He chuckles. "Stubborn as always."

"In truth, sometimes I overwork myself because I think it's all I can do … And sometimes I do it to forget my other problems. Am I doing a good job, Darnor?"

"You are. Trust me, I could never do it all! But you are. You see how everyone looks to you."

"Except you."

He nods. "Rightfully."

I roll my eyes. "You better tell her soon."

He grins broadly, then his eyes soften. "We're practically dating."

My heart swells for them. "Darnor, that's great!"

"Not officially, as she puts it. I took her out for lunch. She was too stubborn for dinner."

I nudge him. "Tell her already." My voice grows heartfelt. "For me."

His cozy eyes connect with mine. "I will. Now, you had better get back."

I prop myself up and slide up the wall, offering him my hand and winking. "The lord had better be getting back to his studies!"

"Oh, I'm overjoyed!"

I burst into a snort. "Really!"

He dusts himself off.

I roll my eyes. "Some lord! Well, Darnor." I dip my head, flourishing my hand. "I take my leave!"

He laughs out loud, but low enough that it's still drowned out by the din of swords over the snow and dirt. The last thing he would want is to make me seem unprofessional. "As do I!"

My voice lightens. "See you soon." And I turn.

"Good luck, Liela. I'll tell you how it goes, and I'm here if you need a rest."

I nod behind his back with a smile, closing my eyes for a moment as I head back over towards Driena and the training fences, opening them to see Driena—her dark hair calls to me as it whips in the gentle breeze, silver sword gleaming by her side.

I join her as she stares unmoving at the training field, eyes sharp and arms crossed. She looks over at me. "What do you think, Liela?"

I hesitate, wanting to say how I feel. But that's me. I believe in my knights, beyond this cold clutching at my heart. "I think we have a decent chance."

She whips her head away. "But I think we have a lot of work to do."

I nod.

"Liela. Orders."

"We can finish this training session. I was hoping to practice our supply runs later this week."

"Of course." She nods, looking pensive.

"Eline!" Driena snaps, at the end of the session, stepping over gracefully to a raven-haired woman. "Your strikes are too high to do proper damage. And you want to be faster." She takes up her sword, eyes hard, but gentle underneath. "Can I show you?"

Eline nods and she eyes Driena with what I think may be fear. "You can, Driena."

I close my eyes for a moment, breathing deeply.

I trained my life for this.

I studied my entire life for this.

I am ready.

I open my eyes, letting them be as fiery as I can let them, and turn to walk down the line of fences, observing the steady progress before me.

It's enough, I keep telling myself.

And yet, there's still no word from Siltheus. It sends a shiver down my spine.

Nevertheless, I stand resolute, knowing that this is our city's purpose. This is what we've always been ready for. As dark as that sounds, in the end we are a fortress.

But to me, we are a people that I would willingly defend, no matter what. Because this is my home, and these are my people.

Caroline Sophia Hamel

To Hold Up the World

Liela

I sit at my desk, hands on my temples. The stars shine so brightly outside, and for a moment, my eyes catch on that.

I let out a brief exhale, trying to dissipate the building heaviness in my chest.

The preparations place so much weight on my shoulders that it's hard to keep track of ... Even with Driena by my side. Even worse, I'm going off phantoms of information.

Between it all, I'm trying to balance Dunet and Myllia. Sometimes, I have to push them aside. It's something I don't like to do, but if I don't ... Then, I can't get anything done. This is the first time I've actually had trouble concentrating on anything—like my mind is being tugged away from my goals and purpose and wondering if it really lies elsewhere. But now, least of all ... is the time to doubt.

I desperately want to slow down. Now more than ever. And more than ever, it's impossible because of the tasks I set for myself and the person I am. I'm struggling to keep up. I just can't seem to get things done, recently.

I don't know what the right thing is.

I shake my head, blearily narrowing my eyes.

Orders for evacuation, food storage and transport, security and scouting, emergency correspondence ... I have all the movements of my army under my grasp. Father is just as overwhelmed with the city's functions as I am and with keeping tentative order. Everyone is on the verge of panic. I can hardly blame them. With our supply and communication lines cut, that makes everything much more complicated.

My eyes feel dry, and my body feels like it's in a dream state, but I straighten my back and focus on the desk and low candlelight in front of me. Again, and again. No matter what it takes, I can never falter. For my people, I would throw away anything. My city needs me. I won't fail them. This is what I worked my entire life for ... built my life on. I will not give up now.

I reach for another report, reading it, clearly and concisely, before giving my signature and writing a purposeful response with crisp strokes of my quill—no less than any other. None of them can be any less meaningful.

It's a hard task in keeping my attention up. I want so much to sleep, or see Myllia, or check to see how Dunet is doing—if I even really do. I should see Darnor, or have a short session of relief and respite with Father to just unload, where we can laugh with each other over our shared stress. But I know that's far beyond my capacity or time.

I never knew stress like this, but I worked for it. I worked hard. So many long hours and so much focus ... that my only real social time was through my work, with my fellow knights. I liked it like that. I admit that this is something that I'm proud of myself for. It's exhausting, but I know the payoff will be so rewarding that I can already feel the pressure leaving me and that surge in my chest to know I did everything that I could, because everything I do extends far beyond me. I have influence and I intend to make the best of it—to use it for good. To protect.

My eyes droop a little and I shake my head roughly. Everyone I know will be safe. That is why I'm here ... It's what I intend to make true. I give a smile, so close to collapsing, like my eyelids. I will come through.

I stir, eyes snapping open after a moment, and I take in the dim work area with a frown and a sigh. I look up blearily to see Myllia standing beside me with a blanket draped around me. I sit up slowly, my back aching. "Myllia?" I rub at my eyes, giving the clearest smile I can.

She casts her eyes down at me gently, her hands twisting the dress at her sides, but her smile is warmly lit, like home. "You fell asleep, and I thought you looked cold." Really, her cornflower eyes have so much depth, that in my stupor, I could get lost in them. "Is there anything I can do?"

I feel a calm settle over my mind with her here. Sometimes, I don't realize how tight I am and how strained my mind is to get everything right. I pause, closing my eyes and forcing myself to slow down and reflect on what I need and want.

Usually, I skip over my needs, but I work better when I don't. While I know I could push through it all, something seems to tell me otherwise ...

Maybe it's Myllia? I know what I want in this moment. My eyes settle on her—so pretty, gorgeous, kind. Her hair is plaited tonight, but with a few curls descending past her fair ears, and she wears a flattering white nightgown with delicate lace etchings over her plump form. I catch myself staring and rub at my cheeks, as they start feeling fuzzy. My heartbeat picks up. I lower my eyes down to her thick legs and catch her ankles. I always thought she had beautiful ankles ...

What are you thinking, Liela? I look back up into her eyes, my cheeks still flush.

"Stay here tonight, Myllia." I know that's all I've wanted for a while. A part of my chest feels empty without her here. If I could, I would always be with her. For whatever reason, that longing weighs on me the most at night. Maybe I could sleep better with her here? It's been so hard to sleep lately ... I just stare at the ceiling, or out the window to the star-flecked majesty of the snow-covered Kalltarris Mountains.

Her eyes go wide, and she brings her hand near her pretty jawline, cheeks a hot red. Her other hand twists her dress by her side.

"Will you?" I ask, failing to understand her surprise, though my own heart feels awfully jumpy and light.

She stifles a short giggle with her hand, eyes twinkling, and glances around with a blush. But her lips soften and her eyes do too. "Of course, Liela. I just thought … Well, you are never so upfront." Her eyes are so clear that it tingles all my nerves. "I am happy that you want me here, though." She touches her hand over her heart. "Liela, whatever you need, I am here. I just do not want to see you do so much by yourself."

I smile gratefully. Then I take a moment, my heart hammering. I had never asked her to stay, even if I've wanted to. My mind still feels a bit foggy. "I can take the couch."

I start to collect myself and hear Myllia giggling hysterically behind me. "Liela, we can share!"

This time, my shoulders jolt and I feel a heat in my cheeks. My skin seems to twitch.

"You do know what you want, right, Liela?" she teases, tilting her head with a shy twinkle to her eyes as I glance back at her.

"Oh …" My mouth feels dry. "I just meant …"

"I know. I want to be with you, is all. You have been so stressed lately and I thought you might not always want to be alone."

"Myllia," I mouth.

"If I am here, then I want to spend that time near you." She leans over and kisses me with dazzling eyes, playing with her hair with one finger. She giggles at the end of the kiss, before looking at me with depth that seems to tug me towards her. Her eyelashes flit—playful and gorgeous, but meaningful, leaving me enraptured … and a little stunned, like always.

"Thank you. You look gorgeous, Myllia." It's so hard to keep myself from looking at her, as I let myself glance at her bountiful curves. She really does look gorgeous in her nightdress, and I wonder if I'm blushing.

I move to the bed, and she gets in next to me. "Liela, you know I cannot take it when you are so clueless. It really is sweet." She gives a compassionate smile.

I turn over, heartbeat too floaty, I try to get it to settle down.

"Good night, Liela." I hear her say lovingly.

"Good night, Myllia," I respond affectionately through the dryness in my mouth.

Myllia

I give a small smile, aching at my cheeks. I rest my hands against my chest, breathing in deeply. Liela is right next to me, close enough to touch …

Tonight, she looks so beautiful. The moon shines over her angular frame and beautiful brown hair that I love. I want to giggle at how modestly she dresses, even if it's still less modest than usual—she's in a nightgown of beautiful dark, forest green silk. I never knew she wore dresses. Maybe it's for me, or maybe it's just when she sleeps alone. But if this is what I get with her, then it's enough.

I'm glad she asked me to stay, and glad at her wholesomeness. I curl into myself, feeling warmth at my core. She can be so unaware sometimes and I love her for it.

It makes everything more perfect just to be with her. Maybe I want more, but this is enough. And right now, this is perfect. I tuck in closer to her, staring up at the ceiling, knowing that she's right here next to me.

I love her.

Rain as Cold as Ice

Driena

The rain comes down.

I let it.

It kisses my skin coldly, soaking into my dark black hair and violet clothing, and trailing my skin. At this point, why not embrace it?

I close my eyes and when I open them, she's there in the doorway, the rain sleeting like a curtain between us.

It's hard seeing my sister. It makes me feel like screaming out, but I want to hide at the same time.

But I stand solid and icy as ever. Who I am.

Joyless. That's what she is. But ... Better than me.

She comes out from my family's home—dark hair and icy eyes that are lighter than mine, from under chestnut-black hair and an azure blue hood. Azure to my violet and chestnut to my black.

She looks older than she is. Straight posture and her eyes keen.

She walks up. Her hand appears briefly from beneath her cloak, to wave, then she's standing in front of me.

"You look nice."

She stares up at me, eyes never straying from mine. My throat twists for once. "So do you." This is how we know each other, and I am all right with it. My lies to Liela and to Darnor were just that. I swallow. At least, they were only half lies.

I don't mind her shrewd, somber wisdom. She's a good sister, after all. Better than me. Responsible. Brave. Kind.

"Ella." Eleanor Kira Tollus. She goes by Ella or Kira with those close to her. The shred of herself she kept. It looks wrong on her now. She's not a child. I would tell her that, but even that's hard, and for once, I'm worried that it would be crossing a line.

Her eyes darken. "What is it?"

"I ..."

"You have enough to tell me, right?" Her words are piercing, but they barely numb me at this point.

"I just wanted lunch."

"I suppose that you did." She taps her foot in the dirt. "You can stop pretending to be something you're not, Driena. You did enough for me. If you can't tell, I no longer have you here."

There are so many things that I want to say, and I stuff them all away, doing my best to look forward. "I never was."

"Driena." It is direct and meaningful. "Lunch? I know you loved Bella's."

"I did."

"You went there for me."

She starts walking past my still form, then turns, meeting me in a hug, but her voice is distant and pronounced. "I never get it."

I close my eyes. "Me neither."

"Then that makes us the same."

Is that what you want?

"I never told you I was proud of you for being under the wing of the Commander."

"Thank you, Ella, but I knew that." I want to smile then, but my cheeks just won't give way.

She turns and I walk behind her through the mud. "You can at least wear a hood. Here." She tosses me an extra hood. "I grabbed it when I saw you outside."

I take it silently, casting my eyes to her.

Ella looks back. Her eyes narrow slightly and she frowns, tapping her forehead with her index finger. "What is that, Driena? You know, you always are so distant nowadays. I miss you."

I open my mouth to say something, but what can I?

She stops, grabbing my hands and lifting them between us. She stares intently; her eyes are sharp, just like mine. "Can you say something, because sometimes I am tired of you idolizing Liela and losing everything else ..." She sighs.

"But I don't." My mouth is dry.

She closes her eyes. "Driena, I get it. I just ..." She turns around and continues.

My feet remain planted, then I move forward, slogging gracefully through the mud and sleet. I sigh. I want to push myself away from her as much as I want to get closer.

I do idolize Liela, but it's more than that. I think she knows that too.

We live in the residential district. I was a childhood friend of Liela's. Things got a lot easier once I became a knight. My family thought it was too hard to rise that far, but I did—no matter how unlikely. Not that we were poor or anything, our life was fine ... And it's still fine. We had enough and our family hasn't bothered for more.

There's a calmness in that.

Something unchanging, even if everything else does.

Bella is in front of me. Just a few blocks from home. It looks warm, but shallow. Creaking in the wind and rain, but sturdy and quaint. It's a family restaurant—one that my family knows. Its windows peek out pleasantly, and the whole thing is framed in homey wood, with an overhang and a wooden porch on the front side.

I move up beside Ella as she pushes open the door, removing my own hood to the small interior—pleasant candlelight, low lighting, tables along the wall, pots decorating the center of it, and some stairs lead up to the living area surrounding the central beam of the room. There's a small kitchen taking up half the space, behind the wall to my right. The owners let me back there a few times, when I was young.

Norma, an older, pleasant-looking woman with curly-white hair, shallow eyes, and a kind smile, sits near the reception desk. Elma, Talli, and Jacob are her grandchildren, working here as a side or full-time job.

Talli sits by her grandmother near the fire—fiery-red hair, a sweet smile, freckles, and a light-green overall dress. They sit by the hearth, behind the welcome area.

Jacob is also freckled, but with dark brown-red, half-length hair, fair skin, and soft emerald eyes, like his sister's. He leans against the waiting area stand, propping himself up on his elbows as we enter. He brings his hand up in a wave. "Ella, Dri, it's been a while!" It sends an unpleasant ripple up my neck. I was called Dri once. Sometimes. Ella stopped calling me that, but some people I know still do. It's a bit strange.

I wasn't always so aloof. I was just like every other teenager once—or I tried to be. Of course, to some people, I am. To Liela and Darnor, I'm approachable. I don't think that makes me a bad person—just different.

I put on a smile. "It has, Jacob."

Ella stuffs her pockets as I look sidelong at her and she glances at me.

"Could you get us a table by the corner?"

"Certainly!" He looks back as he guides us over. "Some time off, Driena?"

"Briefly. I wanted to see my family." A half lie.

"Lucky for you." He smiles pleasantly. "I know El would like it." I think Ella liked it once, but the siblings have names for all their younger customers. I wonder if she likes it now. She just gives a pleasant enough smile when he looks at her.

He leaves us at the table, and I seat myself across from Ella.

"Driena." She laces her hands in front of her on the table, her eyes searching. "You hate that I am like what you've become, don't you? Either way, I turned into what you wanted me to be, and you're a good person."

I remain silent at that, looking over the mature lines of her face, then cast my eyes out the window.

"Tell me something. Please, Driena. You know that I want to listen. What is it that you want? You were the one who told me you wanted to be more genuine and that you

Caroline Sophia Hamel

wanted to be there in all the ways you thought you failed." She shakes her head. "But you're still scared."

I turn, looking out the window. "You're right that I do idolize Liela."

She nods.

"She's a special person. I know there's a lot I could've been. You know I wanted to be defiant and strong. I wanted to prove something and be more than I was expected to be. To me, this is all practical now. I follow Liela ... because she isn't me. She's kind." I turn back to her and her eyes that never stray. I break it off far too soon, but I feel exposed in my words. "Has your schooling been hard?"

"If you don't want to keep talking, then it's manageable."

"Mother says you're doing fine."

"I am." Her mouth sets in a line. "You know I can do anything. You told me that, before you were different. And you were harder on me later, so I would say it paid off."

"Are you struggling?"

"I am. And you told me to take care of myself. I am resourceful, but I did reach out to my professors. I'm helping tutor the younger kids on the side, especially those who don't have as much help."

I swallow, my shoulders falling.

"Like a lot of people," she says, "I get scared."

"I cry sometimes ..." I whisper it.

"Because of me. Liela is like your sister now, isn't she?"

I nod quietly.

Her eyes are fragile, but not cold. "I always thought she was."

"She was the only reason I could do this, and the only way I can seem to repay her ... is by hurting her." My voice is still, and I still look out the window. "I've always thought that's right. But recently, I just wonder ..."

"If it really is? Why do you want to tell her what to do, Driena?"

I look back at her.

"It all comes back to me, doesn't it?"

I only nod.

My heart races a bit to acknowledge it and I flex my hand awkwardly. I didn't think I would want to do this or try. "I think I'm in love ..."

She tilts her head back a little, a thin smile on her lips. "Well, a first." She lets out a scattered laugh, that's partly a sigh. "You told me." She smiles. "I'm glad for that, at least, and I never thought you had it in you. Well, who is it?"

"Darnor."

"Oh, that friend. I remember him a little. But why do you tell me that?"

"I'm trying not to keep secrets. I hate to admit it."

"You're blushing. You might as well be giggling!"

"I am not!" I clench my hands reflexively.

She closes her eyes, lowering her shoulders. "Thank you. Tell me anything, Driena. You know it's painful that you don't want to be around me."

"I know. I don't think I have much time left, though."

"Try. And then, maybe one day, we can do something fun. You don't always have to be hard or push me away. If anything, you lost me more. You overcorrected. You got too uptight. I still needed your soft side, Driena. Your sisterly side. You went from someone so soft, to someone who tried to be someone that you never were. I want a girl's night, a sister's night out. Don't you?"

My mouth is dry, and my hands are shaking. "I do."

She reaches across to grab my hands. "Then don't be scared."

I swallow and meet her eyes, giving my best smile. "I'll do my best."

"You never hide that well around me—that face that screams you're putting on a front."

"Sometimes I hate it. I never think about it, but I do."

"I'll help you let it go."

I shake my head.

"Trust me this once." She cranes forward, hands still placed over mine.

I look, this time more gently, at our hands. "Okay. I can do that much."

She rests back. "Yes, you can, Driena."

She's stronger than I am. Maybe ... maybe I can stop being scared I'll hurt her, and I can treat her like a sister again?

A Place That Does Not Exist

Dunet

I can't go back to the kitchens. Not without Torie. Without her by my side, it would feel empty—like there was something missing. Something straining at the lost parts of myself. And screaming ... for someone I do not deserve.

A comfort I do not deserve.

I feel like I lost something important to me.

And there's nothing in its place. Just emptiness. When I needed to feel something, I could go there. When Liela was gone, that was my haven.

And now ... I don't feel like I can.

So, I make my way to the only place that hasn't changed.

To Eriena and the stables.

Out of everyone, I don't feel like a burden to her.

Maybe it's because she can't talk back. But to me she can, and her eyes are so kind and so understanding. Gentle in a way that reaches across to me. Maybe she's a pony, but she's my friend, and sometimes I feel like she's the only one who understands me; who can share without expectation or hurt.

Who cares about me for me, no matter what.

I creak the door open to her pen, and she whinnies at me, moving forward and nuzzling into my chest.

I wrap myself around her muzzle, stroking my hand through her mane. "Hello, Eriena." My voice is fragile. "I'm tired."

She whinnies quietly, nuzzling me closer.

"You have no idea how much I hurt. I feel like I have nothing left at this point except you. Here." I laugh just a little, for real this time, pulling out a carrot.

Eriena nibbles at it and I giggle.

I wipe at my nose, sniffling. "I needed that. I think I only feel sane here, with you ..." I trail off, her eyes large and gentle as they look at me, feeling like they're connecting so deeply that it strains at my chest. "I know you deserve better."

Her eyes seem to tell me otherwise.

A smile forms on my lips. "If I could be myself again, I think you'd be the reason." I slump in the hay. "I just want to hide here for a while. Then we can go out." I look up at her from my slumped position, my chest rising ever-so-slightly and a lump in my throat. "Or, maybe, we could go now?" I rise up and stroke her flank, before pulling her up, unsaddled, and whispering in her ear. "I'm sorry I made you wait. You're such a patient girl." I want her to be free. As if she knows me better than anyone, she starts moving, and I let her carry me, smiling to myself and to her as she does.

Caroline Sophia Hamel

She's quiet, but it's a quiet we share as we break out gently in the sunrise, mist dancing around us like a long-forgotten dream and a past life.

But for once, I feel just a little free.

Caroline Sophia Hamel

To Turn Away Warmth

Dunet

He finds me.

I hate that he does.

Under the castle stonework, as usual. The rain drips between the stems and leaves of the shrubs and bushes and trickles along the cracks in the stonework behind me. It seeps into my hair, matting it as it blurs the air around me. I can only see a short distance—it hides me from the world. My hands are freezing. This is the first rain in weeks between snowfalls. It licks my hands with an icy tongue. I never really care. It can have me if it wants to.

His boots are the first thing I notice—the refinement of a lord, in their modest brown leather with eloquent straps, but not a pace to match. Yet, there's something about him that I can relate to—that I want to latch on to. It makes me tempted to draw my eyes up, but I don't want to look up at him, as pleasant and welcoming as his eyes and his words are.

Lean and well-muscled, shoulders narrow, but broad enough to draw attention, smooth, distinct jawline, slightly pointed nose, elegant-brown hair, pleasant, deep blue eyes, and a refined, but laid-back quality—a composure that would be what I imagine people his age would consider handsome. Another thing I don't get. I can tell when people look at each other in adoration. I don't think Liela would ever choose to see that. Frankly, I never quite understood

Liela and Myllia, even though I could tell they were perfect for each other.

Not that I would care anyway, even if I did.

I look up at him, not caring to hide my glassy eyes and the shadow of my face.

I would rather him see me dead.

And I want to tell him to go away.

He cracks a grin at me. "Mind if I sit?"

I hesitate, peeking at him from between my fingers.

"You know that you're hard to find? But I guess I know the feeling ..." His eyes are kind again, if far off; they are still sparking. I wish mine were too.

I turn back into my hands and whisper. "Go away."

"What was that?" he says as he kneels. He brushes at his shoulders a bit with a frown, sighing at the water. "You know, I think it's a bit cold for a daydream." But then, he looks into my eyes with too much generosity in his smile.

I turn my face, avoiding any chance of him seeing me. "I ..." My breath shakes, because I've never been so outwardly hurtful in a way that was intentional. "I don't want you here."

"Dunet, no one deserves to be completely alone. Is it all right if I ask you to look at me?"

I squeeze my eyes hard. "You already did."

"I know. But I just thought that I'd try. I know it's pointless. Your sister's stubborn too. She's also very avoidant."

I bring my hands down slowly, feeling no less cold, but enough of me wants to see him. That desire barely exists. Still, it clings to the only person who might understand me. But I want to shrink back ... For me, this feels dangerous.

I want to be alone. I want to be hollow. Again and again, I tell myself that. It's better that way.

His smile is gentle and coaxing. I laugh just barely at his eyes.

He swivels his head, raising his eyebrows. "What is it?"

"Liela said you looked like a puppy." I giggle, a small crack forming in my shell.

Darnor frowns. "Not my favorite compliment." And then he smiles with a laugh. "But I suppose it's all I'll get." He shakes his head. "Oh, Liela ... I wish she'd come up with anything different."

I look at him directly, with a smile. "It suits you." Then my face clouds over again and I turn away into shadow. I try curling up, feeling the ice-cold grass, ground frozen nearly solid beneath a sheen of water.

"Dunet, I think you would catch a cold like that. I know Liela wouldn't like it."

I clutch at the grass with numb fingers. "I know."

He moves over, leaning against the stone wall and under the bush with me. I wonder how he hasn't gotten bothered enough to leave. He should leave me here. "Is there anything I can do?"

I let the silence stretch.

The rain breaks a little, replaced by a cold breeze that snakes through the branches. In my head, it's silence. I can't help letting a shiver go through my shoulders, but I continue to stare forward. My lips feel parched.

"I understand if there's nothing you can say." He stares forward too, wind ruffling his hair. "I was like that too. It took ages to feel like myself again ... to feel at all alive ..." He sighs, leaning his head back. "There were so many things going on in my head. That no one cared. That I was worthless. That no one would miss me. I felt so empty. Stuck. I retreated and put on my best smile everywhere. Maybe people would believe it. Maybe I could do something by being here. Not hurting anyone. Of course ..." He trails off. "I was. Myself and others." He looks back at me. "I thought about ending it more times than I could count. I know it feels like no one understands you. That's why I want to be here." He grins, "I know, I don't seem the sort. I suppose that's the thing with us. No one questions that we're happy. That everything is all right inside our minds ..."

I curl up further, trying to deflect his words, even as I catch them up with numb hands, before letting them fall and break. Because no one can understand this emptiness ... I want it to be only mine.

"Hey, Dunet. Other people help. Talking helps. And I know you feel hollow, but maybe one day, you can let yourself cry."

I squeeze my eyes shut and push up from the ground.

"You can come to me, but I won't tell you to. And, Dunet." He points to himself. "I got through this. I know you can too. I also know you probably feel guilty about Liela."

I nod.

He shakes his head. "Don't. You *can* be selfish. Learn to live with it, is all ..." He grins again. "I know *I* have, and my friends never stop teasing me for it! Really, it will be the death of me. But ignore me, I'm morbid sometimes ..."

"I hate help."

He looks back patiently at me, now sitting on his knees.

"But not because of you ..." I lower my eyes.

"If I told you that it wasn't a weakness, would you believe me?"

I shake my head. "No. I want everyone happy."

"And is there something I can do?"

"Leave." It's small and cold.

"Are you sure?"

"Yes." It chills me. I don't sound human. I'm too gross and too awful to deserve his help, no matter what he says. There's only this me, who's empty and hides. There's nothing beyond this broken mind that only wants to please and take and is too afraid of losing.

"Your feelings aren't a burden ..." I listen to his feet crunch on the frost and close my eyes.

When I wake up, I'm home, a blanket around me and a fire burning before me, steaming cup of hot cocoa in front of me.

I feel the smallest spark from the fire. Something that still reaches me ... someone who doesn't deserve it.

I wish I could smile, just this once. A real one.

I close my eyes, pretending to sleep as Mommy kisses me and changes out the mug.

Then I hear her rest into an armchair by the fire.

I crack my eyes open. The floor-to-ceiling windows cast the beginnings of starlight and moonlight over the sleeping city and the edge of the room—the ceiling sprawls above me, and the entrance to the kitchen and dining room look dark. I must've slept for hours. The fire casts long shadows over the floor, wavering and dancing darkly in my eyes.

Home has stopped feeling warm.

Mom opens up a book. Her crystalline eyes draw from its pages behind full lashes. She sits back in her perfect posture, her plaited brunette hair draped over her plum and turquoise night dress, but there is a tiredness about her I never realized—lines below her rosy, polished face. I thought she was always perfect—that she held the world and took care of us in it. To anyone else, she does.

I creak on the sofa and squeeze my eyes shut.

I hear Mom's padding feet and she places a gentle kiss on my cheek, brushing my face with a steady hand. "You had a long day, darling."

My smile lifts at her touch. "I'm tired."

"You must be. And I want you to dream. Your sister's friend found you. You must be starving, so I'll get you something when you wake."

I feel a twisting in my stomach and want to hide again. I'm a burden.

Did Darnor come back for me? He must have.

I was stupid to think he would leave me alone like that …

She strokes my cheek lightly, her touch refined. "You're a beautiful girl. I will help you through anything."

I reach out, grabbing her wrist, but then I look away, drawing my hand back. "Are you proud of me?"

"Always."

I nod. "Why?"

"Because you are my special girl. All I need is that."

I breathe in gently, facing the pillow. "Where's Liela?"

"Studying, I think." Her voice never feels quite right in these instances. I spent so long not noticing.

"Do you hate her?" It's a terrible thing to say, but I'm just starting to notice.

I feel her breathe in. "Another time, darling, but ..." I hear the weariness in her voice for once. "I love both my children very much."

I smile lightly. "I wish she knew. I miss her ..."

"I know you do. Dunet, I am still here. I am your mother."

"I know." I sigh, so she can't hear, "You're everything to me." Turning over, I sit up with a radiant smile and move to hug her. "I love you, Mommy!"

She strokes my hair. "I love you too, darling."

I know that I have the most wonderful mom and the most wonderful family that I could ever ask for. They deserve better.

But, for now, I'm content to cling to them.

She leaves me with a smile and comes back with a plate of bread and cheese. She sets it down with a warm grace I treasure and have known my entire life.

"Thank you, Mom."

"I will always do this for you." She comes to tuck me in. "Call me if you need me."

I nod with a smile like a blooming flower. For the first time in what feels like such a long stretch of pain ... I feel safe and warm.

And it's not with Liela ...

I stay up for hours.

At least, I try to.

To see Liela.

I fall in-and-out of sleep, barely trying at this point. Do I even care to see her? But my heartbeat is quick, instead of muted like it often is now. But it's just my heart. Everything else feels drained.

I hate her getting back late. Why does she delay her return? It's cold without her ... although, it can be cold with her.

She always gets back late now.

I hear the squeak of the door and a pad of feet that aren't Liela's, along with hers.

I draw up, blanket still around my shoulders and buttery hair cascading in unkempt tangles. I don't bother trying to rub the sleep from my eyes anymore, like I used to do so playfully.

It's Liela and Myllia, holding hands. My eyes go dark at their closeness, and I turn away, feeling cold. I look back and see that rosy red on Myllia's cheeks, as she grips Liela's hand and smiles at me, hand creasing her dress.

I breathe, then smile groggily back.

She lets go Liela's hand and comes over to me. "Dunet! Liela and I, well ..." She looks over at Liela and blushes again, holding her lavender dress.

I smile back kindly. "Myllia, I know. I'm okay that you're here, really."

"Well ..." She squeezes my hand softly. "I thought I would at least say good night."

I nod, part of me wanting to burst out in a smile, but part of me is squirming, wanting to look away. "Good night." I look over her shoulder at Liela, who's flexing her fingers and straighter than she normally is when around me. She meets my eyes and ...

Her eyes look broken and torn now, but only when they're on me. She should hate me, instead of missing me. My presence must feel like a burden to her.

Suddenly, I wish I could cry.

But I'm empty. Tired.

I sink back into the couch, turning towards the fire.

"Good night, Liela."

I can't deal with it all right now.

She comes over and kneels next to me.

Then I feel her hugging me. I don't feel anything.

Not anymore.

"Are you all right?" There's so much worry in her voice, and it grasps at me pleadingly.

I grab her back, clutch her, and that at least is genuine. "Yes, I am, Sister." I lighten my voice—try to make it cheery.

It must sound fake.

But Liela pulls away and smiles. "Good. I love you so much, Dunet."

I smile back. "I love you too."

I wonder if she picked up on it, and is just hiding now.

At what point will I truly break her?

Liela

My heart wants to lock.

Should I stay?

I think I should. I want to.

But ...

Do I?

I feel pushed away, but her last reply and her smile brought enough lightness to reassure me she's okay.

Isn't she?

This uncertainty tears me apart.

It's like she doesn't need me.

I tell myself that I can try tomorrow.

I move back and grab Myllia's hand, almost ghost-like, still looking back at the couch.

We move back into the hallway under moonbeams, then into my sparse, neat room.

Myllia turns as we enter, closing the door.

"Did I do the right thing, Myllia?" My heart pounds with her in front of me, even as I feel detached.

"You always do, Liela. At least you try, and that is what I love about you."

She moves forward to hold me.

"Was she okay?"

"I cannot say that for her." She tilts her head against me.

I nod.

"I know some things feel hard to say." She pulls away and looks up at me with a giggle. She raises her shoulders. "But you look gorgeous tonight." She comes closer to me again and my heart pounds. "Can I?"

I nod and we pull together, her lips touching mine, gentle as a fall leaf.

"Liela, I think I am feeling a bit naughty."

My heart tumbles, in a knot.

She presses her forehead against mine. "As much as I want that, I do not think you are ready. Anyway, I like a slow romance." She puts a finger lightly to my lips, then grips my hands. "Sometimes I think we should sleep these things off." Her arms go back around my neck, and she kisses me one more time. "Good night, Liela."

Myllia

She was so tempting.

I really wanted to lean into her. Honestly, I am ready for every step. And in the moonlight and starlight, I can see every vulnerable detail of her angular face. She's so lovely and so unsure of herself. I just want to wrap my arms around her and kiss her. I want her to take me to bed. I want to feel every part of her.

My heart beats wildly with that desire.

I stare at her beautiful profile and the gorgeous brown of her hair. I'm always still falling for her, again, and again. My core heats up. I didn't know I would want sex so soon in our relationship. Knowing me, I would ask her soon. Honestly, I really don't know if I want to marry her first or have this. I thought all I wanted was marriage. And I think she might say yes. It makes my heart skip a beat. But I'm still one for tender, slow romance. Yes, maybe a little straightforward, but I don't want to ruin this calm pace. I know that's just an excuse for my heart's longings, though.

I can't take it sometimes and I wonder if it's the same for her.

I love her, so I know that it's only natural.

I giggle in the bedsheets, Liela beside me.

Maybe I should ask her out on an official date sometime? I know she still hasn't asked me if I'm ready to be introduced to her parents. I know it's scary, but I wish she would. I want to give her time, though. I sigh lightly, unsure if that would ever happen with mine.

But, I have almost everything I need right here. All I ever wanted.

I always wish things were better with the two of them. Still, there's enough brightness in my life that I want to believe things will get better.

Caroline Sophia Hamel

The Absence of Perfection

Liela

"She was outside in the cold, Fenor! She could have frozen."

I can hear a calm response from Father.

"No, that's bad enough. Didn't we teach her? She shouldn't be doing things like this at her age. It's rebellious."

As I get closer, Father's voice hits my ears again. "She's too smart for that. I don't think it's that." His voice drops. "I'm more worried about her."

"What's gotten into her, Fenor?" Mother sounds irritated.

Father sighs. "Calm down, Fern. I know, it's stressful, but I'm sure she didn't mean anything by it."

I stand outside the door to my parent's suite, sprawling high with a large bed, white and forest green sheets, a few posh armchairs, and an exit on one side leading to a grand balcony and the other to a large bathing area. They invited me into this discussion, but I hesitate to join them immediately. I bite my tongue, feeling the need to defend her, but I know that I always make things a lot worse when I'm around Mother, so I let Father handle it. Plus, this conversation feels uncomfortably familiar to how Mother lost her faith in me.

"Stressful? You know I don't think she meant anything by it. I've just had enough after Liela." I hear Mother sigh. "I did what I could to make Dunet comfortable."

"I know you did," he says soothingly. "But you need to see this situation through her eyes."

"Do you think it was nothing?"

"Maybe, but we can't just ignore her."

I step out from behind the wall at that moment, feeling a little awkward.

Mother looks up from between her hands and frowns at me. "Liela, do you know what's going on?"

It takes me several seconds to weigh my words, wondering if I do know or not. "No." I look between them, avoiding eye-contact. "She said she was all right."

Mother purses her lips. "I'm not sure if you've been paying attention."

"It's okay, Fern." Father stops pacing and gestures at me with his hand. "Liela's been under a lot of stress."

I nod at him thankfully, though I feel tense at the familiar notion of being blamed for my lack of awareness.

"Your mother and I are figuring out what to do."

"Maybe we ought to limit her time outside?" Mother lifts her tea to her lips.

"We can't ground her, Fern."

My lips feel a bit dry. I want to defend Dunet, but I believed her when she said she was okay, so I don't know what I'm defending. Still, I want her safe.

Mother presses her hand to her forehead. "This is beyond me."

"Do you have any thoughts, Liela?" Father asks.

"I just want her happy and safe. I'm sure it was just an accident." After all, Dunet follows every rule to a tee in ways I couldn't even do.

"True," Father says, nearly smiling when he adds, "I must admit that even my influence hasn't corrupted her."

"Fenor, this is serious."

"I know." Father nods solemnly. "I'll need to have some sort of talk with Dunet about safety. But she always listens to our rules perfectly." Father frowns again. "I'm sure she will continue to do so, so I'm not sure what the issue is."

"She was probably just playing," Mother suggests after a pause. "I don't think she understands how deadly the cold can be."

I nod responsively, agreeing with Mother for once.

I want to forget it happened, because I know Dunet would never willingly endanger herself. She cares too much about us. I'm certain she knows that, if she were to vanish from our lives, our hearts would shatter into a million pieces. The damage would be beyond repair.

Mother squeezes the bridge of her nose. "I think we should all come together and have some family time."

I feel a slight drop in my stomach; a familiar nervousness. Often I can loosen up, but at times I just feel tense when both my parents are around. It's for Dunet, though.

"Liela's been busy a lot." Father walks up next to me and ruffles my hair, like he used to do all the time. "I've missed you."

"True," Mother says, looking a bit weary. "She's been hunkering in her room."

"Understandably," Father corrects. "She's a busy Commander."

I look at him gratefully. "Thanks," I whisper. It's not like I consciously avoid my family, do I? I've just been preoccupied with everything going on.

Mother continues to look solemn. "I propose we do something special."

I look up at her and I'm surprised that this grateful feeling extends towards her. Even if she doesn't treat me very warmly, at least she goes out of her way to care for Dunet. At least she loves her.

I work side by side with Mother.

I find it strange that she was the one who proposed this. It should've been me. I know that Mother cares about

Dunet too. She's sweet and loving to her. I know I shouldn't be thinking about that now, but I miss that.

At first, she's silent. When I look up at her, I hear a sigh escape her, followed by the words, "You know I worry too."

"I know."

"I worried about you the same way."

I look away, not knowing what to say to that.

She shakes her head. "You were a difficult child for me."

"You mean I am a difficult child for you," I retort.

"Liela," she says dangerously, "I'm just worried. Dunet hasn't displayed all your tendencies. I didn't think I'd have to worry."

I narrow my eyes at her, before blanking on her meaning. My tendencies?

Regardless of my understanding, I don't ask her about it.

"She's perfect," I say on impulse.

"Liela. This is one of those things that bother me. You never pay attention to what you should."

"What?" I squint at the carrot peeler in my hand.

"Don't question me with that tone." She shakes her head. "The one thing I'm grateful for is that you won't argue with me on this."

I go stiff, sending an immediate retort in my defense, "Why would I?"

"Liela," she says sharply, "you don't need to rebut everything I say. I said I was happy you're here."

I breathe out, cooling off my temper a little. "I want to be. I'd do anything for her."

She goes unreadable for a moment. "Dunet asked about us."

My blood goes cold.

"And what did you say?" I ask, trying to hide my uncertainty.

"That I loved you."

I close my eyes, breathing through my teeth. "Of course, you'd say that to her." I wish you'd just tell her you hate me, I think.

"I thought you'd be appreciative for once."

I don't reply to her for a moment. "I am."

"Then you don't have to question my motives every few seconds."

"And you don't need to find every moment to criticize me!" My hand shakes and I nearly drop the peeler.

Setting it down on the counter, I hold my hand to steady it. "Sorry. Thank you for being there for Dunet."

She nods in acknowledgement. "I don't *lie* about loving you."

I squeeze my eyes shut. "Just, don't talk about that right now. Dunet's the priority." I keep myself composed, realizing I feel too shaky. "I need a break." I push away from the counter, heading quickly to my room. Once there, I pace the floor several times, my fists balled up and trembling.

I get worked up far too easily.

I can't tell whether I want to cry or punch something.

Maybe Mother loves me ... Maybe it's an obligation? But I have no doubt that she dislikes me. If I was born to another woman and we were absolute strangers, Mother would have nothing to do with me.

I crack my knuckles, breathing out shakily as I try not to cry, my brief spike in anger leaving me. As soon as that fire dies down, I hold my breath and resist the urge to give into grief.

Why do I get reactive at the worst times?

My hand shakes as I reach for the doorknob. I can hold myself together until after the dinner, can't I? Mother expects that. My fear of her anger overrides my fear of breaking down.

Just think of Dunet.

Dunet

I come to the table last, looking around unsurely before plopping into my seat.

None of them say anything at first, looking at me with possible concern or hurt, maybe. I rehearse my excuses in my head, though they all feel tiny and weak.

"I wasn't sure when you'd come," Dad says. I don't quite get his tone and resist furrowing my brow to instead smile. I think I guessed right, because he smiles back at me. "I cooked for the first time in eons! We all did."

Liela laughs jovially. "It was quite the time!"

I duck my eyes. I wasn't there, of course. I feel a bit empty and alone. Though, it wouldn't matter if I were there.

Father winks at her and I look back and forth between them.

At least Liela was there. At least she got to spend time with them. She never does.

Liela turns to me, a smile on her face. I try to mimic one back. I hope it comes across genuinely.

Mommy clears her throat, squeezing Daddy's hand.

She looks me over and I'm unsure what to feel. She's only ever shown me warmth. I look between her and Liela, conflicted by my new knowledge.

"Your mother wanted to do something for you."

"It must have been scary being out there," Mommy says with a level voice.

I nod. I didn't really feel scared. I didn't really feel anything. I was just grateful to find solitude, and I didn't occur to me that I should be scared or that I should miss my family.

"I'm glad you're okay. I couldn't bear to see you hurt." Her eyes look watery. "I know it's not really a special occasion, but we all agreed as a family that we'd pull through for you."

My heart drops a little. They shouldn't have taken time out of their lives because they were worried about me.

Dad laces his fingers together on the table before speaking. "Liela, will you do the honors?"

"Certainly!"

Liela leans forward. I don't quite keep up with what she's doing.

She uncovers a dish that she has set in front of me, then she pulls me into a shaky hug. She whispers to me, "I'm … sorry I haven't been there." I just nod. "We wanted to celebrate you being okay."

My breath stops. My vision feels a bit blurry, and I want to bolt.

I don't want to be here.

Mother comes over and plants a kiss on my forehead.

I feel uncertain at the cake in front of me. I don't deserve this.

Mother pulls away, returning to her seat with a smile. I focus on maintaining a happy expression.

They look at me expectantly. I hide my face a little. "Thank you!" My voice is squeaky.

"You're certainly welcome," says Father.

"That you didn't botch the ingredients!" Liela's exclamation seems almost planned.

"I did perfectly fine. In fact, it was so good I may have eaten some!"

Liela laughs raucously, "You would, Father!"

I look between them, realizing I should laugh too, and I do.

When I begin to eat, I don't taste my food, and I can hardly focus on the conversation, though I don't try as much as I maybe should.

It's exhausting, timing my laughter and expressions to match theirs at all times. I feel so far away. It's lonely here.

Mother casts her gaze to me occasionally. I ... think I actually felt comfort with her there, when I was home.

For them celebrating me being alive, I feel strangely apathetic.

I wish I could give them more than this.

When the meal reaches its end, I trudge over to Mother and she makes room for me on her lap, stroking my hair.

Liela looks at us blankly for several moments and I pretend to close my eyes. I have just realized that they've been avoiding each other the whole conversation. I'm bothered by this, but I can't bring myself to be upset at either of them. I don't pretend that I understand them well enough to pick a side, and I never would because that would be wrong. But the tension still makes me nervous.

I start pushing myself up.

"Are you uncomfortable?" Mother asks.

"No." I shake my head.

She nods and unfurls her arms.

I get up, looking back and forth from the table to the hallway as I trudge off.

Then I sprint the short distance to my room, my heartrate quick and my breathing rapid. I'm wide-eyed, as I stare around the room, collapsing under the bed in a shaking ball for no real reason.

I shiver frantically, whimpering a little.

It lasts for a while. It's nice in here, though. It's calmer. Quieter.

And I settle down after a while, looking intently at the grains in my bedframe. My mind is empty, apart from that.

I turn over after a while, crawling out to grab Ceilia, before going back under.

There wasn't anything particularly threatening happening, but somehow, I feel safer this way.

Caroline Sophia Hamel

The Drop of Hope

Myllia

I knew when I received the summons that something was off.

It leaves my heart racing, and I hold it as I take the stairs.

My parents know I would be near Liela now—at least that would be their best and most accurate guess, since I told them I love her. Or, at least, they would know to find me here.

I close my eyes, not knowing what to think. Maybe I should've had him meet me here? After all, Sam is a guest. But something makes me hesitate to bring him here—it's like having my parents in my personal life, something I never had to think about.

Sam Corfell is our family's private messenger.

I know that if my parents sent him, then it must be important.

My eyes catch him, heart falling. He's young, with an unblemished face—after all, he represents my family. His slick blonde hair is swept to the side, his skin fair and clear, and limbs and hands slim and delicate. One of the more well-paid servants under my father. Still, I always found it surprising that he chose someone so young.

He grimaces when he sees me, sticking out a note. "From Lord Hansel Ornel Laundra … To you."

I take it slowly, trying to hide my shaking hand. "Thank you, Sam."

He turns his head away. "Don't mention it. Sorry … I never liked you."

My mouth gapes at him.

"Really, I-I am …" he stutters. "I still never wanted to deliver this. Sorry." He bows slightly, then scampers off. He turns back a moment later and meets my eyes. "I'm sure Nieda misses you."

I mouth, "Thank you."

He turns again. I stand motionless for a moment, then I rush up the steps, my heart pounding. I reach the top, time slogging, and find my way down the hall to Liela's room, closing the door and sinking my back against the wood to catch my uneven breath, squeezing my eyes shut for a moment.

I approach her bed slowly, after grabbing my letter opener off her desk first, and sit, heart pounding, midday sun glaring across the white bedsheets. The world looks so far away and small through the window.

I turn my eyes back to the note again and breathe, closing my eyes for another moment, before they settle on the message with as much strength as they can.

My hand shakes as I open the note with my petite, silver letter-opener. I take several breaths before I unfold it, not knowing at all what to expect. And then, I look down.

Myllia Courtney Laundra,

Your mother and I have discussed. As you know, I was disappointed and made that clear. We put a lot of effort into your marriage with the right man. We think that you are being hasty and rushing into something that you do not understand. Commander Cordre has an admirable station, but we do not support your marriage to this Commander, however respectable this young girl may be. I am personally disappointed that you did not listen to our side and come with an open mind to consent to a very fair marriage. Your mother and I may disagree on a few specifics, but this is final. We drop your title, your inheritance, and all your holdings. The Laundra estate will be reserved to us. As it stands, this gives you what you asked for. You are no longer formally of the Laundra house and have no influence on or bearing over the Laundra name. And any formal acknowledgement of a marriage to this girl will be rejected. I will begrudgingly give you that I respect your desire to attend Clenine, but I think that is as well misguided. I may have overlooked that, if not for your other desires.

With my fairest apologies,

Lord Hansel Ornel Laundra

I stare blankly at the note.

This was not what I wanted. I wanted to show them who I could be ... I wanted to repair all of this. I thought I did the right thing ...

My breathing picks up and I clutch my chest as it spirals out of my control, rapidly rising and falling. I hold my chest, trying to calm myself and steady my breathing.

My hands are shaking as I sit there.

For a moment, I want to disappear into a fairytale again and it's then that the tears start falling and can't stop.

Suddenly, I find it hard to tell Liela that I failed.

That, in this, I'm a failure.

Even though I did what I thought was right, it didn't matter.

I can barely breathe as I sit forward.

I promised myself not to do this, though. I promised myself to move forward. And so, I'll tell her—tell her that I got disowned by my own parents for loving her, for standing up for myself and wanting the best for myself and reaching for the only thread of a relationship that was possible ... I thought to want them still in my life was selfless.

Wasn't it?

I wish I could redo it. But what would I say differently?

I said the only words that truly mattered. I gave everything that I could have for this one moment.

Maybe it was too quick? I know I should've started sooner, but I wasn't ready sooner.

Even if they wanted that for me, it was clear that they never approved of my marriage to Liela anyway, no matter her station, because of what that means to them. I was stupid to think her being Commander would be enough for them. Nothing would've.

I don't want to choose between Liela and my parents, but I can't choose who I love.

I lean into my tears, with the small hope that they'll come around.

If they can't respect my choices, that's all right with me, but I can't stop loving Liela. That, at least … isn't a choice. Not in a million years.

We do not decide our hearts.

Liela finds me later. I sit on her bed, in the middle of her sparse, neat room.

I gave up hiding anything from her.

As torn apart as I feel, I am not conflicted about anything. I know where my place is, and I know my next steps. But in order to take them, I just need Liela here.

I give a shy smile. "Yes, I found my way to your room." It's still a weak smile and my lip quivers.

Liela's eyes soften, and she moves quickly over the remaining distance of the room.

I wipe my eyes with a strained giggle. "I did it, Liela … Well, I did what I needed to do." I choke on the end. "You know, I wanted to talk about it with you before now."

She falls to her knees before me and I catch the full force of her olive eyes, making me breathless and dizzy as she reaches for my hands.

"What happened, Myllia? You look like you've been crying." Her face looks so torn that it hurts.

I giggle again and it turns into a hiccup, then a staggered laugh. "Do not do that to me, Liela!" I shake my head, still somewhere in-between a sniffle and a giggle. "I cannot take it. In truth, I wanted to be who you saw in me." I squeeze her hands back and smile weakly.

"Myllia?"

"I told you that I wanted to be the best version of myself for you. Without you, I would still be stumbling through my life." A sob wracks through me.

Liela moves up onto the bed next to me and I let my head fall onto her chest, her heartbeat bringing me peace. She strokes my hair, like I see her do with Dunet sometimes, but even more tender. "You're doing just fine, Myllia."

"I am enrolling in Clenine." I sit up and look at her. "I want to help people and understand them. If I can, I want to heal the gaps in their hearts."

"Myllia …" Her eyes soften. "You are far too kind."

"Maybe, but I feel so strained right now. I think there is far too much for me to handle. I … I revoked my arranged marriage." My voice shakes. "But it is all okay. I told myself it would be. I just hoped …" My eyes start moistening again.

Liela hesitates a moment, then pulls me back.

"Here." My voice is small as I give her the note.

Her eyes dart over the page and I hold my breath. "Myllia …" she breathes, her own voice seeming dry as she clutches me.

"I hoped that I could have them for once. That maybe, we could work something out. Maybe we could have become close."

"I'm so sorry." She holds me tightly.

"Liela." I pull back and look at her eyes, getting every last inch of her gorgeous dark hair, her beautiful olive eyes, her sharp, plain face that looks gorgeous, like everything else on her, the slenderness of her, and all the calm comfort. "I made this decision. I will always move forward, for you and for myself. No matter what, I will use every last one of my strengths that you saw in me. You were the first one to truly see it, and I promise that for you and for me, I want to give it back."

She shakes her head, her eyes wide and soft.

"I lied when I said that it did not matter when they neglected me. It did matter. But what matters more to me right now is that I do not give myself up. I promise that for them too, I will be happy. And I hope that one day, they will see that ..."

My last words come out as barely a whisper, but I cannot help looking towards that possibility.

"Like you said they would. I will make them proud, Liela. I will make you proud. And in the end ... if I have done this all knowing that it is for the future I want, then it is worth it." I sink against her chest, resting my palm against her breast and the heartbeat underneath. "You know that all I ever wanted was true love like in a fairytale. Well, you are my fairytale. But, Liela ... I realized something else too. My fairytale was only the beginning. You ... you taught me that I could walk on my own. You taught me that I could live my own future and that what I could do for others meant something. Because of you, I found what I love, and it just so happened to be with who I love."

I listen to her heartbeat, my eyes closed, and I whisper, "You are my dream, my fairytale, Liela. But my dream has grown so much larger than I thought it could."

She stills for a moment. "Myllia ..." she breathes. "I ... wasn't sure what to think, when you told me you would tell me after you moved forward to be your best self. I know ... it may be a lot for me to take in, but I love you too and I'm proud of you. Myllia, you are a wonderful person. I told you this a long time ago … I think it was around when we met, but I know more than anything, that you deserve so much better."

I smile silently, because it was from when we met.

"I want to be there for you, like you are for me. I hope that I can be."

"You already are, Liela. In every way that matters."

"What do you need?"

"I want to stay with you tonight." My heart flutters, feeling nearly ravenous for once. "Can I do that?"

"Of course, Myllia."

I look up as she looks away. "Liela, you know you are gorgeous. I wonder if you could ever say no. You know, you give me everything that I have ever wanted."

"Myllia, I just thought I could tell you that I got a bit scared." Her voice drops. "I was afraid of what you meant earlier. I never looked for love, but a small part of me was afraid of what you meant, now that I've found it."

"Liela. You are far from possessive. You do not have it in you, I was not going to leave you because of this. You are part of whatever dream I have."

She meets my eyes again. "I know that now, Myllia."

I look away. "I wish I could have come back with something better. But right now, can you just hold me? I … I think I am a little tired."

Liela looks at the sheets, then looks away, her face blossoming red.

"Do not worry, Liela, I know you are not ready yet." I turn my eyes up to her. "But I know that there is a lot going on. My parents declined it already, but in time, there is something that I want to ask you."

I think that I can hear her heartbeat thundering.

I rest the tips of my fingers into my cheek, leaning into them, still sitting on the edge of the bed. "But not yet. Liela … What are you comfortable with? I can wear whatever." I swallow.

"I will just go change." She ducks into her bathroom. "But just normal nightclothes."

I bring my hand to my heart, feeling its frantic beat. I'm also too scared. But soon—so soon, I want to ask her to marry me. Everything else can wait, but that is the one thing that I have always longed for most. I was never sure if I could have that moment—if it would ever be in front of me …

But I could imagine no one more perfect to stand in front of me on that gentle altar of my dreams.

Liela

I feel panic rise along every point of my body, but at the same time … goosebumps.

Why does this feel so frightening?

I look back at my reflection and frown, like I often do when I'm alone with a mirror.

Myllia deserves better. I'm glad she saw something in me, but I don't know how. I'm not desirable, nor do I know what to say.

I just hope that what I say is always enough.

And how could I not know that Myllia was going through so much?

I just want to do something to help! I bite my lip, feeling helpless again, just like when everything went wrong with Dunet. Except this time ... What is there that's in my power to do?

Being Commander ... How does it even help in these situations? Sometimes I feel like I can do nothing.

I thought I was strong.

I know. I scrunch my face. This isn't about me. This is about Myllia. But I feel just as lost as I felt with Dunet. Just as powerless ...

I press my hands to my face and look up in the mirror, heart picking up again.

But I breathe, picking out the least suggestive nightclothes I have—dull-white linen shirt and pants that barely look feminine in their shape, almost baggy, not that I have many feminine clothes to begin with. I hate looking at myself and I always want to turn away.

I wish that I had Myllia's confidence sometimes. Not my confidence, but hers, in how she can just not care sometimes.

I hope she can forgive me for trying to look so modest. I'm just not ready yet … my heart pounds too much … is too frantic. I know she'd never mind, but still, today of all days, I wish I had it in me.

I take another breath, biting down on my lip again, and change reluctantly.

It's not like we are doing anything, just sharing a bed to sleep, but my heart is thundering … because I'll want her to keep staying here with me each night, because she has nowhere to stay, and it scares me to have her with me as much as my skin jumps in excitement. But it's the least that I can offer her right now.

She is no longer a Lady—not officially. And that means that everything was taken from her, but whatever I tell my family—my cheeks grow hot—or if I tell them … I know that they would never turn her away. I know I'm fortunate that while I have some fears, they are unlikely to be the same ones that Myllia faced with her family.

I'm glad she at least has that comfort to fall on. They will treat her like family, and we have enough for her.

Myllia

Liela comes back with modest plain white nightclothes, making her look like any other teenager, and I smile under my hand, already having changed into a flowing black nightgown—something a bit different for me and I wonder if it catches Liela off-guard. I slip into bed, looking back at her.

Her eyes reflect the sobriety in mine, as she climbs in next to me.

"Good night, Liela," I murmur, with a quiet love, sending all the heartfelt meaning I can behind it. I squeeze my eyes shut, trying to accept those cold words I read as true and real, but not at this moment, with Liela.

"Good night, Myllia ..." She reaches over to hug me, leaving her arms around me, and I bring them back.

Because I want a world with just her in this moment.

I let the last few struggling tears dissolve until morning, when I will face my fate, with Liela walking at my side, supporting me ...

Pain Grasping at a Heartbeat

Myllia

My eyes look puffy in the mirror, as I wipe away my halfhearted makeup attempt.

They're red from crying, still moist, but dry, in that they have nothing left.

This is Liela's mirror. In her bathroom.

In her bathroom …

My heart races.

I want to kiss her and make everything go away.

I want so much to drown in her.

Just her.

Just us.

I wonder if she can hear me crying. If she had. I know, though, that she would know that I'd want her with me.

I sniffle and the door opens.

I turn around with a tired smile. My hands are shaking and the tears threaten to fall again.

It's like I never really had any parents to begin with. I never even mattered in the end.

And what's worse is part of that is true because of my love for Liela.

I would be fine enough if this happened from me standing up for myself and only that. Maybe a bit rude, a bit disrespectful, but who I am—my heart tears up and my eyes sting—is not a part of that.

So, why?

Liela stands before me quietly, her eyes askance.

I walk over to her—my bare feet trembling—and kiss her. Desperately.

I pull away, in turmoil.

She grabs my hand, knowing what I want, and leads me gently over to the bed, sitting before me. I shift onto her lap, legs twining around her as my arms reach back behind her head and she falls for me onto the bed.

I'm still crying as I try to forget the note from my parents.

So distant and so final.

I am not theirs.

It should feel like freedom ...

I stare into the depths of her olive eyes, as my mouth takes in hers, her hands loosening my dress, as mine play at her bra. I know I'm in the wrong mindset for sex, but I want it.

I have wanted it. It's unbearable, more than I thought were possible, or that I was capable of.

I slow down, untwining my legs from hers and pulling my mouth back, looking directly into her olive eyes with a renewed calm. She looks so beautiful and pretty and fragile, her dark brown hair loose from her ponytail and cascading in strands over the upper portion of her small breasts, sweat droplets forming on her wiry stomach, and the heat of her just under her sky-blue underwear, half off of her and slipped partway down her hips ... I want to take her ... to soak into her. My core is so warm with desire for her.

I laugh. I look like a mess, clothes half off and bra falling from my shoulders, rising with tension. Liela's exposed chest rises and falls slowly, calling out to my heart. I want so much to kiss her again, but I can't do this now.

Not to her. I smile. I want this to be special. There is always later.

Her eyes are still shining, brow glistening, as her eyes ravish my body, sending a shiver up my exposed skin. She opens her mouth, as if to talk, then closes it again, blushing profusely.

She looks so mature right now. Her body lithe and her agile form spread tall over the sheets. Every line of hers is beautiful. From her lovely hands, to her pronounced collarbones, the length of her gorgeous legs, her small and firm, mature breasts, and finally her eyes.

I pull my hips back, a jolt running up my spine. My body twitches at the absence of her heat, and I sit beside her on the bed.

She sits up, turning to look at me as her shy eyes fall slightly. "What is it, Myllia?"

"It is just ... I want this to be special."

She rests her hand on my bare leg, then as I shiver; she takes it off and slips it into my hand. "This is special, Myllia."

"I want you so much, Liela. It is just hard not to fall in, when ... Just remembering those words tears my heart in two. I thought I could forget it with you. But I want to be with you, for you, not to forget anything."

We sit there for several long minutes, our breathing slowing.

"You could never hurt me, Myllia. But you're right. I don't think I'm in the right mindset tonight, either." She shrugs. "I'm not ready, but I think soon, I will be."

I say it quietly. "I think we'll know."

She nods, then rests her head against me, her hands rubbing my back. I lean back into her. "There's always tomorrow. I will love you then too."

I giggle, looking down at what could've been, but knowing we stopped at the right place. "I love you, Liela. I want you like that desperately."

We sit there pleasantly, light gently moving across the room. I close my eyes against her. She's so close. But this is fine for me now. Just a little longer.

Caroline Sophia Hamel

When You Are Met with Something Empty

Dunet

I hear Liela's door creak open. I squint my eyes, knowing it's rude to eaves-drop. That squirming sensation is there, but so small—so diminished that it no longer matters. I peek out to see Liela slowly closing the door, eyes runny and looking tired.

I hesitate, tightly bringing my eyes shut, and then I force them open to confront her. Because something about how she looks—how frail she looks and how heavy—just makes my heart and soul sink. It's one of the first things that I've felt in such a long time.

For the first time in however long … I'm drawn to someone.

"Dunet …" I hear the sniffle just barely, as she tugs on a smile. "Good morning." It echoes painfully strained and absent. Her eyes are baggy and dissonant, like she'd been up all night.

I grab my arm reflexively, but my own eyes betray just the tiny hint of uncertainty. "Is something wrong, Liela?"

She looks towards the door and her chest seems to constrict. "It's Myllia …"

"Oh. Can I do anything?" I try to bring my voice up, if I can still do anything, but I still feel distant, like I'm in a far-off tunnel. She's tugged to her again ... So far away from me.

"I wish there was something that I could do." She looks to me with shattered eyes. "She would want to see you, though."

I meet her eyes. "Okay." My breath comes out pained.

She kneels in front of me. "I love you, Dunet. I'm sorry, but ... there's going to be more going on for me. I ..." She shakes her head, sniffling again. "I ..."

I quiet her by hugging her back. "I love you too and I love Myllia. I want to help in whatever way I can."

She nods, and gives a small cough, as if her throat is too tight to get the words out. "Thank you. Dunet ... I'm sorry, again."

I stare off at the wall. I should be the one who's sorry. Always.

She pulls away, smiles at me, then transitions into a stride in her forest green uniform. Once again, I never feel like I can reach where she is. Once again, I'm just in the way.

I want to help Myllia, but only barely. It's like a whisper in my mind—like a thought swept away in a frigid wind. I'm in an empty room, huge and dark, and everyone is outside of it—I'm alone with only echoes.

Do I want to see Myllia? Will I care?

Of course, I will. I must. Because I love her, don't I? Doesn't she mean a lot to me now?

Maybe not, or maybe she does? But I have to do something, if only for her.

Or to lessen the guilt that comes with doing nothing.

Even if I don't know what to expect, I feel at a standstill.

I push open the door after a brief knock, hearing a loud sniffle. Myllia looks up.

"Oh, Dunet …" she stumbles for words, wiping at her eyes.

I stop in the doorway, feeling small, and holding my hands behind my back. "Myllia."

"I know I am a mess. This time"—she scrunches her eyes, sobbing, and she bends over— "I really am. I thought I did everything right. For me and for Liela and for you."

I lift my feet that shouldn't be heavy but are. I want to run away. My feet twitch to run.

But I sit next to her stiffly.

She raises her head, her eyes a puddle and just a little misty. She sniffles again. "My parents disowned me, you know."

I gulp as I see her lip quiver.

"I wanted to be me. That was it. To finally do something with my life. But also … to just be with … be with

Liela ..." Her face scrunches up and her breathing starts to pick up.

I bend forward, giving her a hug, my own mind still stunned and my gaze swimming. I didn't think I could cry now, but damp tears meet the bedsheets from my wide, parched eyes.

"So, you see ..." Her voice is lost, but her breathing has slowed. "I just ... I thought. I know it is hard for you to understand, maybe. I just thought I could have it all."

My mouth is dry, and it sticks together as I talk. "They left you ...?" It's a small voice, that singular notion barely registering.

"Yes."

"Why?" My own voice trembles, a tiny part reaching out and wondering.

"Because I loved Liela ... And sometimes people do not think that's okay." She seems to hold onto me tighter, as her breathing becomes erratic. My own touch is so ... so ... there and not, but I'm hoping I reassure her.

"They ..." My breath catches. "But you love her ..."

"I do, and I know that is okay. It always was and it always will be. That is why I am grateful for people like you, Dunet."

I breathe out, then I clench my eyes shut.

"And there may be the fact that I broke out of my marriage, wanted to enroll in Clenine, and enraged my parents for standing up to them. I ..." She laughs and sobs at the same time. "I cannot believe the looks on their faces. Part of me feels bad about it. Part of me feels guilty. But if not for me loving a girl, loving Liela ... I do not think they would have let me go. I do not think they had it in them for that ... but for this, they did. And because of that, I know that I should not feel guilty. My father's words make me want to cry. I still cannot believe I saw them ..." She sniffles again. "But I did." Her voice steadies. "I did see them." She pulls away and looks at me teary-eyed.

I stare back, my eyes clearer again. There is only one thing I can say to her, because it's true. "You are my family, Myllia."

She puts a hand to her mouth. "Oh, Dunet." And her face contorts, as she looks up at me—her eyes barely hold behind her tears. "Thank you. I know ... but you do not know how much that means to me ..."

I nod, knowing it's barely anything, but it's at least something she needed. "You're as much my family as my sister and my parents." I hold my smile. "I want you here."

She nods several times, her face falling apart and distorted sobs coming through the hand over her mouth. I pull her towards me, holding her hand and squeezing, like she would do for me, and she squeezes back, her hand larger and soft. My eyes are dry, the bare pinpricks of tears just under the surface ... and they fall ...

If this is all I can do, then it's something ...

But I stare out.

I'm empty.

Beyond this moment. And even now. Even now. Myllia deserves better.

I wonder if my tears are real.

I blink, drawing myself back to reality. To Myllia's reality … And I hold her harder, closer, but gentle.

This moment is for her pain, not mine.

So, why do I want it to be mine? Why am I screaming out for her?

Why do I want to push her away? I should want to hold her closer.

But like every other moment, I want to disappear.

I want to be by myself.

I want to leave everyone alone.

In the dark.

No.

I want to hide in the dark.

I want them to be free, even when I no longer care about them and do nothing for them …

Because I'm selfish, but nothing seems to push them all away.

Morning of Promise

Myllia

It's been so many days since reading my parents' letter and it's still hard to not feel numb.

I remind myself again of why I did this. I know it was the right thing to do.

Liela and Dunet help, of course. I treasure their words.

They're my family, more so than my parents ever were. I smile silently, sitting with my hands folded in my lap, on Liela's bed.

I find myself sitting here a lot, just wishing for her, and letting the hours flow by in silence.

I watch that time tilt through the window, between gray, blue, and white—city in the distance, beyond the castles' walls.

I know this is far from healthy, but I can't help drifting away. This is how I had used up my hours for much of my life—waiting, dreaming, and longing.

And there's no denying that all I want right now is Liela. To feel her.

I fall softly onto my side and close my eyes over her bedsheets, imagining her here with me.

Then my eyes flutter open to the white sheen of the world that seems to pause for me.

What will I do?

I know I can and refuse to give up the choices I finally made. I promise myself that I'll be ready for Clenine. That dream is still there, and it's waiting for me on the horizon.

I wish it were here, though. I could use it right now.

And can I really imagine living off Liela—Lord or not? I know I must take up my own life now. I promised myself that.

I slip off the bed and move to Liela's sparse closet, which is taken up by the clothes I'd managed to keep. Father sent a final courtesy, as he put it. Maybe it's lust or maybe it's the new pit in me, but if it wasn't for Liela's family, I don't think I could bring myself to change into anything right now—not that I ever really cared about modesty. Today I wear a sky blue dress with white ruffles. I don a sweater from the closet—a light gray one with white fleece at the cuffs, neckline, and waistline.

If anything, I can at least wander off—not that it feels any less numb to get out. Maybe I do not daydream quite as much anymore, but it's a hard habit not to fall back on.

I look at Dunet's room for a moment as I leave Liela's, wondering if she's all right, even though I know she'd be gone right now. To know that she considers me family really does mean the world. I wish I could find it within myself to be there for her right now. I smile a little. I know I will be soon enough.

I find myself drifting down the stairs and out into the courtyards of the castle, snow falling lightly. I shiver, but I spent far too much of my life daydreaming in courtyards and gardens to care. It's like a miniature snow globe or a dreamscape. A wonderland where I could stare off into my fantasies. I let them take me so far.

My breath frosts and I smile as I find myself in the courtyard I shared for so many months with Liela. It has been my favorite spot since that day. The pond is frozen over today, flowers and grasses near the water frosted, the tree by the water sagging with snow, and the ivy-covered entrance keeping guard like an enchanting portal.

I close my eyes, imagining it in spring.

It was so much simpler then.

I move to the waterside, crouching, and resting there, holding my knees.

I clutch my hands to my chest, feeling that pressure. My face is so tense.

I wipe at my eyes with my sleeve. I knew I would find myself sobbing if I came here. I blink my eyes, knowing it's no use, as I bend over and let the tears fall. It's a soft cry, but it still feels harsh. Why would there be any reason for things to sting so much now?

It's such a relief to cry right now. I've been crying so much lately.

But one thing is certain: I lost the will to spend all my time daydreaming. Nothing can really bring it back. Still, I wish the lines could stop blurring between my desire and what I really need right now. Not that they can't be compatible, but just that nothing seems clear.

It does really—everything does. But at the same time, all I ever want to do is cry and kiss Liela. Feel Liela. Entwine her and be held by her.

Just Liela.

I touch my lips again and they feel cold.

But I know that's an okay thing to feel.

I promise myself that I can ask with a clear head next time. I know we'll both know. I would hate to pressure her to make love to me. Knowing her, she would do it. For me.

I lower my hand and my lips part delicately.

I lean back, watching the dreamy sky for a moment.

After that moment, I decide to go to town. Not to shop—I would hate to spend Liela's money, Lord or not—but I need to do something to keep my mind occupied until my new courses start at Clenine.

It crosses my mind that maybe I should get a job. Otherwise, it would fall on Liela's family. They can afford it—by any means, they could afford that and more—but I find I can no longer sit idly. I wonder what it would be like to work. What would I do?

I could work at a dress shop, maybe? If I had to do anything, I would love that. Or maybe a sweet shop?

Something to do while I study.

My mind drifts to the future. I wonder how hard it could be ...

Regardless, it's something I want to do. I find that it's the easiest decision in the world, really.

I roll over on my side in the snow and frost, giggling and fluttering my legs. A new excitement shivers through my heart.

Yes, maybe things look so unknown right now, but I've never felt so free.

It makes me smile brightly, despite every new pain in my heart for the love I never had from my parents. My mind and heart feel clear at this moment.

So clear.

I rise and brush at my dress.

Then I hesitate. One of the few regrets and things I will miss is that I can no longer call a carriage, especially if I ever want to take Liela on a date. Carriages always were one of the things I loved most—to see the world glance by.

I would have to walk. But I know that, compared to anything else, that is not much to ask of myself.

With as much delicacy as I can offer my new place in the world, I head off to town.

~

My legs ache when I get to town.

I'll have to get used to this, but every second of this, I want to laugh. My throat still throbs, but there's so much in front of me.

I move off to the side of the thoroughfare, bustling with throngs of people and carriages and numerous tracks through the muddy snow, the shops and stalls along the sides bursting with activity, even in winter. Yet, I notice a certain subdued nature. Even with Liela as commander, the difficulties in communication and trade seems to have hit. Somehow, I feel outside all of it, though. I wonder if I should feel more panicked than I do.

I feel panicked for Liela, because of all the pressure on her, but I never really took the time to think about much else. I wonder how I've always been in this bubble. What does that feel like, to be on the outside? I wonder what they have to worry about that I don't.

It all feels so ... new.

I find a bench at the side of the thoroughfare to sit and catch my breath. At least, I was smart enough to not wear heels, but my silver-white flats are caked in mud. I frown at them, chest deflating just a little. This is just something I'll have to live with. I slip them off, massaging the tender soles of my feet for a moment and feeling that sigh through my limbs. They ache. Burn. I wince at my ankles, so glad not to have worn heels. My skin looks uncalloused and unblemished, like most of me.

I look up, taking in more details now. About a quarter of those out dress in finery—many drawn on horseback and by carriages. I'm in that quarter and, for once, I notice just how much I stand out. The rest are in various levels of casual clothing and work clothes of a far less sophisticated make. They look less delicate, and in more of a hurry.

I wonder if I looked oblivious before.

I frown at them.

Some of them are dirt-stained, but on the main thoroughfare at least, most look like they have enough. I wonder what and if I should do anything. Would it be okay for me to mingle?

I slip back on my shoe, lifting my other foot as I slip that flat off, and massage my throbbing ankle and sole for just a few more minutes. Then I find it in me to stand.

I make my way to the dress shop first, opening the shining glass doors to the dim, but soft radiance and rows of racks, streams of light falling through the skylights, candles lit and protected at the ends of each row, a few antique mirrors, and the dressing rooms at the edges. The gowns call in every shade.

I make my way past them to the back, fingers tracing the racks and fabric with an ingrained longing for anything beautiful. I love anything like this. This is part of that fairytale that I wove—a part I will keep. I'm still a dainty, elegant girl, with a love for dresses and everything pretty. I get so much confidence from it. Even if I was not aware of it before, I really do pride myself in my presentation.

As I approach the back, I catch Alice's eye behind her desk—dark-haired and gorgeous, with her pale-blue eyes, slender face, thin frame, and mature smile. She's in a lush and sensual dress of pure black, leg slitted, and she wears a lavish opal necklace. She's in her mid-thirties, and I always looked up to her. Really, she's beautiful beyond compare. A darling, she's called herself, and I agree.

I smile lightly. "Alice."

Her smile is luscious and pronounced behind her scarlet lipstick. "Myllia. It has been ages!" Her lips blossom.

"I know! It really has!" I glance around. "Actually, I was looking for a job."

"Oh!" Her eyes widen, then her lip quirks. "Well, I can say that I'm surprised. I never thought a beautiful young woman like you would need one."

"Oh, I just think it's about time I get one."

"Now, I like you, Myllia, but I cannot say an amateur will do. I know you have the passion." She leans over the desk across her palm, legs crossed, her v-neck and thin dress straps catching a sumptuous angle and drawing my eye subconsciously. "I'm not quite sure. I would love to have you, though! I would adore the help and I can say you have an eye for style." She ruffles through her desk drawers, scarlet manicured nails catching the light. "You can fill this out if you're still serious and look it over carefully. But, Myllia, I can't promise anything. I would jump at it if you were qualified." She traces the desk with her manicured nail and shrugs. "Business."

"I will do just that. And I really do understand that I may be an inconvenience."

"Well, if you're right for the job, you would of course get in." She winks at me. "Want to chat? Catch up, by any chance?"

"I would love to, but maybe at another time."

She brushes her wrist at me. "Well, I hope to have you stop by sometime soon. I would buy us drinks."

"I certainly will. I want to apologize, too. I will not have the money to buy anything for some time."

Her eyebrow seems to rise to the ceiling. "Are you all right, Myllia?"

I laugh as lightly as I can. "Maybe not completely, but I can cope." But my hand drifts off to my dress. "I apologize, but I do not feel quite ready to talk about it yet."

She nods slowly. "Take care, Myllia."

"You as well, and I promise to be back soon."

I make my way out the glass door, chest feeling a bit heavy. Maybe I should have stayed and talked? Distracted myself a bit. Gotten drinks when she got off. I can still turn around.

I doubt she would understand, but I cannot deny that I feel called out to join her.

I close my eyes, leaning against a wall for a moment.

Another time. I really do not feel like it right now.

I open them and look back onto the snow drifting on the passers-by. There's so much weight to stand and my chest feels heavy. My mind does too. I think I ought to go back and rest soon.

I feel tired. Too much. I know it's not just from physical exhaustion.

But I want to make at least one last stop, maybe two.

At the sweet store. And then I might try out a pastry stand.

Then I can go home.

To Liela.

Her.

Right now, I let that motivate me to keep going. I can be with her when I get back.

She always reminds me of why I do things. Her and Dunet.

I hope I find more reasons at Clenine.

I think I will.

In fact, my heart is sure of it, tugged like an anchor to dreams I didn't realize I had.

The sweet shop is next, and my smile bursts a little at the thought of seeing Helin. Yes, Alice is a nice older woman with experience whom I look up to. She's gorgeous. But Helin is a bit younger. They're both amazing people, of course.

I tuck my hands into my coat pockets on the way over. It only takes a few minutes before I see the cute, little building on the street corner, tucked in near an alley—a colorful yellow and white pattern that looks cheery and inviting amidst the snow. The windows are wide and behind them is the delectable sight of chocolate and other homemade candies. I smile through my frosted breath. It looks so appealing right now.

A bell rings as I open the door into the bright shop, and I see Helin perk up. I smile at her. In another corner, there are two girls ogling a display of candy.

I move over to her behind her desk, and she smiles brightly at me, hazel eyes alighting from under her pixie hair. Creamy skin, sharp nose, and soft, firm lips. She dresses similarly to last time I was here, with her sleek-black, open suit, except she has a rosy, white-pink shirt on this time, bright strawberry pants, and lofted orange shoes.

I admit that Helin makes my heart flutter ever so slightly. I do have somewhat of a crush on her and after doing it so much myself, she flirts with me. I feel a bit bad for Liela, who never had the knowledge or support system I did of girls being in love. I seeked it out and I was able to connect with three women like me: Nieda and Helin, who are lesbians, and Alice, who likes both women and men. Really, sometimes I think it's a wonder and it's only my love of reading and access to rare books that I even recognized it. My heart skips several beats. At least I have a talent for falling in love with the right people. I giggle to myself at how oblivious Liela was until I told her directly. It still sends a chill through my heart.

Maybe if I hadn't fallen for Liela, I could've possibly seen myself with Helin, or with Nieda. But neither would have been able to fill my heart in quite the same way Liela does.

"Myllia!" Her voice comes out swectly. "I haven't seen you in forever."

"I know, Helin! I really did miss you."

She gestures to a stool for me to sit and swivels into her own chair. "Please."

"Thank you, Helin. You know, my life is a whirlwind lately. I really could wind down."

"Really?"

"Yes." I sigh.

She leans forward, elbows on the counter, but she looks at me sidelong. "Your girlfriend?"

"Yes ..." I trail off. "You knew?"

"I thought."

"Yes … her." I trail off mistily. "And my parents … and my life."

"Sounds like you have a full plate."

"I really do."

"Anything I can help with? I love it when you visit, and a friend is a friend."

"What if I told you I was looking for a job?"

She turns to face me and smiles. "Then I would be overjoyed. But I could never guarantee it." She winks at me, crossing her legs casually under her chair. "You're my favorite customer, after all."

"Helin," I laugh. "Really, I know I am not perfect for the job. I want to work with you, though. You know Alice in the dress shop?"

She nods.

"I asked her too."

"Conspirator," she whispers.

"I know."

"Myllia, good luck. I will be right beside you."

"I lost all the support from my parents."

"Then, Myllia …" She gets off the stool and wraps her arms around me gently. "All the more reason to support you. No one deserves that, especially not you."

I nod with a small lump in my throat, and hug her back. "I know. Thank you." Because I need a hug from a friend who's not a lover or her sister, even though I think of them both as friends. Sometimes it can be nice to get one from someone else who cares. And now I'm deciding to make the world outside Liela mine too.

"Now that I think about it, you would be perfect here. But not because you're hurting." She moves back into her seat. "You really would."

"I can let you think some."

She nods. "That's probably best. I'm biased." She gets up and moves behind the counter, coming back with a neatly wrapped box. "I was saving this for your birthday."

"Helin, you never had to do that." My heart implodes at her kindness.

She presses the package into my hand. "For you and Liela. I know you'll need all the support you can get. I can tell how much you two love each other. And her sister is adorable."

I can't help smiling at that as I delicately unfold the package. My heart wants to melt as I see her effort and my eyes glisten at the edges. "I think you did too much." I whisper.

"I did what I wanted. Liela didn't seem the type for jewelry, so I tried something different."

"This is everything to me, Helin." My eyes start to water more, and I wipe at them.

"I just thought it was what you wanted."

"It is. You know me too well, Helin."

She shrugs, but her smile is so sweet and kind. "I know you would want to pick it out, but for women like us, I want someplace special for you." She leans forward, pointing to the note. "Isabella's. She was hard to find, but when you're ready, you'd feel right at home there. She sells rings and she's married to another woman."

I look down at the card and the gifts, my eyes swelling. "Thank you." It really is a beautiful gift. A beautiful honey-gold locket for me with three blank frames and a more practical, but equally beautiful silver pocket watch for Liela with a frame on the inside of the clasp. If we could get portraits done somewhere … Mine has L & M etched on the inside top and my eyes soften at the final touch. With that is a card with the name of Isabella's shop and her district. I clutch it to my chest. "This must have cost a lot." My heart sinks a bit, searching her face. "How did you pay for it?" I know she can't afford things like I can.

"I got a discount." She breathes out. "And a little bit of savings. Alice helped me too. We're friends because of you, and I told her that I wanted to do something for you."

I hold it clasped to my chest.

"It's worth it. You've been my friend for years. I look forward to seeing you more than most customers, Myllia. If anyone deserves this, it's you." It sounds like the most genuine thing coming from her.

"I don't want anything in return."

I hold her hands and squeeze them. "I will always think of this, but never do this again for me. It is perfect, though."

"You're going to make me cry too. You have a way with that."

I wipe my eyes again and laugh. "I think I must."

"What now?"

"I was going to try one last place."

"Myllia, what do you want?"

"Oh, I never told you …" I take a breath and close my eyes, still not fully comprehending the magnitude or reality of what I had decided to do. It still hits me like I'm breathless every time … in the best way. "I applied to Clenine. They have a new program. I want to help people heal emotionally."

"You're wonderful! And a little predictable in your unpredictability. Come by later this week and I'll let you know my decision."

I get up, feeling a little light-headed, but my step is lighter as I wave back at her and exit out the door.

I take one last stop at the pastry shop I'd visited with Dunet—white cloth over the tabletop at the side of the cart facing the street and light gold and ruby tapestry catching the light snow. The same kind woman from last time sits behind the counter—her beautiful smile graces me from under her wispy, white hair, and wrinkled, clear blue eyes. I immediately took a liking to her, especially with how sweet she was towards Dunet.

"Hello, dear. Anything I can help you with?"

"The peach pastry please." I smile at her pleasantly.

She smiles back warmly. "I remember you. You came with such a nice, lively girl."

The corners of my mouth lift even more. "You remember?"

"Of course, dear. I love getting to know my customers." She frowns. "Though I would've liked to see the little lady again."

"She is my friend's sister. I am sure she would jump at the chance to come back!"

"Do tell her I said hello."

I want to 'awe' at that. "I will. You know, I was just curious if you had any openings?"

Her wrinkled eyes seem to spark. "Well, not at the moment. But I like you, dear. I always appreciate help. Why don't you give me a way to contact you and I'll speak up if I need it?"

"Of course." I reach into my purse, grabbing parchment and a portable quill and ink. I loop my name eloquently over the parchment—just my first. I cannot bear thinking about my family right now, and it's not like I still have any connection I can claim. I pass it to her. "This is a friend's address. She'll find me." I feel a bit too self-conscious to write Liela's name. I wonder if it's a bit too much. I wouldn't want to startle anyone or make them feel intimidated. Unfortunately, I don't know whether and where I should address myself as anyone, anywhere, or with anyone. Where do I belong? Physically, really. I know who I think of as family, but I don't know what my future holds.

She frowns at it for a moment, but then looks up at me and smiles. I put Helin's business address. I really don't know what that implies.

"Thank you, dear."

She gets the pastry out of the case, and I reach into my purse again to pay. She smiles at me one last time as I take it. I felt like buying it from her. It wouldn't feel right not to. Although, I frown. Will I have to ask Liela for money soon? I admit, I've paid more than I should've since being left. I have no idea how to manage money and the finances my father left me with are running out. I laugh at myself. Maybe I'm a bit pitiful, and a bit naïve ...

I'll get better, though. For Liela, at least. I'll have to get better for myself too.

I cut off a corner and savor it. It's so delectable and sweet. I look up at the swirling snow and milling crowds as I eat. Truthfully, they melted away from my conscience as I'd walked around. A blur. I can still be oblivious and out of

Caroline Sophia Hamel

it sometimes. When I forget to pay attention ... the world fades out. I splay my fingers to my cheek as I eat, observing the crowd. It's a little ... fascinating. To watch the crowd. I feel drawn to them, but apart, untouched by a newer urgency that feels so hard to comprehend. Those people are busy or furtive or dirty. What should I make of everything? How should I place myself in this world?

I know the first step is Clenine. I will meet so many people who would have never entered my daydreams had I not stepped outside my old comforts.

I dust off my mouth at the last bite and sigh.

I suppose I can try a few more visits. After all, I'm committed to being my own person. I'm ready to do something with my life.

And I can and will try whatever I can to be the best person for myself.

Then for others, by joining Clenine.

I want to.

I will.

Gazes That Hold True

Dunet

I want to run out to her.

I want to.

But I'm held here.

She rides back on Vel, turned in the saddle to Driena. Her figure is sharp and graceful, hair jet black in a way that's too beautiful. Her eyes are stinging ice, face set and hard, even in its cut prettiness.

My fingers curl into fists.

If there's one person I hate, it's her.

She took Liela from me.

But wouldn't it make sense for me to blame Myllia too?

Maybe.

But the two are different. To Liela. Myllia and I are different, too. But Driena—I can see something between her and Liela that I want. I usually avoided her, playing innocent like I always did when she saw me. Her jaw would always be set.

She was there long before Myllia. Liela had her when she didn't have me.

It never bothered me until now.

Maybe I can't bring myself to push anything on Myllia, but Driena's different.

Her gaze meets mine coldly and I go stiff.

I never really understood what Liela saw in her. She looks at her the same way as with me—almost.

Driena glowers at me. I don't know the reasons.

Maybe it rattles against my skull, that she knows me. My mind.

I know she knows that I'm the cause of Liela's fears.

I know she knows I'm not innocent. She probably did long before now.

Her eyes tell me they know everything.

She'd offered me kindness in the past, but it always seemed a distant kindness. She would look from me to Liela. It was like she was taking in my soul.

It's like that now.

I had to pretend to be cheerful around her. It was easy enough ... at least when I still had Liela. When I was all she thought about.

I want to calm myself, but my eyes, which are normally absent, boil. I never thought I could feel this way to anyone but myself. I must remind myself about what I know. That she's probably a much better person than I am. For sticking with Liela. That's the type of person who I should've been. That edge of anger recedes in an instant and I duck my head.

I don't hate her. I hate myself for even thinking that I could hate her. Looking back at her, I can see that she's a beautiful person.

Did I jump to something I shouldn't have? But even if for some reason she did hate me … she would deserve to. Ice snakes back into my eyes, locked far deeper than hers, so nothing can breach them.

As her gaze pierces me, I want to look away. I feel small again.

What can I hold against her?

She's everything my sister needs. I know she must be constant and that she must be more than she seems.

Who am I to judge?

She turns a smile to me, nevertheless.

The stiff grass and frigid wall spread out behind them. The wind slaps my face, nearly tearing it. I let it rip at my gray-white dress.

Liela sees me, her eyes subdued. She rushes over to me. "Dunet, you must be freezing!"

I frown, only now drawing attention to the fact I have no coat. I hadn't had a mind to bother.

I look up at her, my voice dry from disuse.

Why did I come outside? Because, for a brief instant, I didn't want to be alone. That instant is closing, and I want to shrivel up again. Away from both of them.

Liela turns away and I think her fear for me took away any apprehension that she had to be near me.

Somehow that makes my heart feel just the barest amount of warmth.

Driena dismounts, crossing her arms and frowning as she looks between us, but then her mouth sets into a thin, kind smile.

I smile back—my lips quivering.

"I should leave you two."

"Driena, it's all right. You can stay."

"No." I can swear I see a crack in her façade, and I cock my head slightly. Yes, I still keep my childish charms out of habit, or maybe I can't control them? Her eyes almost look ... sad. Broken? Distant?

They're hard again before I can blink.

"I'll see you later, Liela." She smiles gently, a look passing between them, and she draws her horse to the stable.

"All right, Driena," Liela sighs. She then cracks a grin. "See you later!"

Driena rolls her eyes and I feel a pit in my own stomach, gripping my hands hard behind my back.

I want to be alone.

Liela looks back to me, her eyes tender.

I find my voice. "I'm not cold. Really, sister."

"Are you sure?" Her voice is painfully consoling.

I twist my wrist. "Yes."

Her face softens a little.

"Liela …" I hesitate for a moment, voice caught from what I want to say. For a moment, I wonder if I will.

She looks up and down my face.

"I'm glad to see you," I say.

My shoulders release. They were so tense. But I still hold my hands at my sides.

"Dunet." She stops. "Me too. You know, I missed you all day."

Those words are probably false, but I nod anyway.

She wraps her arms around me, and I clutch her like a baby. My throat throbs for some reason, but my eyes are dry. I feel stiff against her. Her familiar warmth.

Sometimes I think that she's all I really have left.

Sometimes I wonder what I would do … if I couldn't envision her face. The thought of her presence holds me back from the knives I want to sink into my chest.

I know that I would break Liela, but I can't stop thinking about it. I don't even know where those thoughts came from.

I do love her, though.

More than anyone.

She brushes my hair delicately. "Want me to take you inside?"

I nod.

She unwraps her arms. "Give me a minute." She goes inside the stables, and I curl my arms around my waist, wanting to sink in a fetal position.

Maybe I can run off before she gets back?

I don't have the strength.

I wonder if Myllia would be with her later. It makes my blood chill.

If only Liela could just forget about me.

Part of me wishes … what if it never happened? I'd never wish that on my sister, but what if?

Would she be miserable?

What if it was just the two of us and the whole world vanished?

Would I have changed too much?

Maybe I'd kill myself and leave her alone. Maybe it would be too painful with us together now. Somehow ... I know I would do the selfish thing and leave Liela alone.

I block that out as best as I can, covering my ears. It never helps.

Liela comes back. Time seems to stretch whenever she's away—it always feels painful. Time never ends. As long as I'm here, it will continue for me.

I feel like I'm viewing the world through a tunnel.

I barely remember half the things around me now.

It's all like an echo.

All meaningless.

How did I collapse so fast?

She wraps me in a blanket and smiles down at me. I tug it closer and smile up at her with as much false light as I can manage.

My fingers shake around the blanket.

I let her tug me towards the castle and I'm glad when she remains silent.

I study her face that still contains the hope I threw away. It makes my chest feel less constrained to know she's optimistic. If she weren't, I would've broken her. Every day that she hopes I heal, it softens the blow just a bit to know she doesn't notice how far in the dark I am.

She looks far off, her face drawn, and I know it's for Myllia. It should be for her. It's a small comfort that makes me smile, even as it makes my chest feel just the slightest bit emptier than it already did.

I know she's been crying. I should care more that she's worried about Myllia. I should care more that Myllia's hurting.

The world has no place for me. My heart locks at the notion that she might one day realize it, and I wonder if I should shield my heart or let the darkness come crashing down and hurt her.

I could drown in peace without her, even if it were torturous to break her. I broke her once. I can break her again.

There are days when I so desperately want her to tell me everything is okay, though. It nearly breaks my lips to tell her. It's why I hide from her.

She tucks me into bed, and it's then that I finally shiver.

She smiles at me. "Do you want me to read you a story?"

I turn away so she can't see my face, and close my eyes. "I do." My words feel stiff now. I know I'll have to work on that. I scream at that effort.

She kisses my cheek and I stare off out the window, clutching Ceilia to my chest. Ceilia, my plush rabbit, feels like a remnant of me. She's a reminder to move forward and smile … and I do. A small one, as I hear Liela's voice. Because today is one of my worse days. I don't know why. It just is.

I curl further into myself.

"There was a girl who breathed magic."

Not me.

"She gave the world smiles."

Not me. I squeeze my eyes shut and tune it out. Her stories are painful sometimes, because I can see myself in half the ones she chooses. Me as an ideal. Occasionally, me as I am. I know which ones Liela believes.

I drift off into a black void that's just a bit lighter than the one I'm in.

In it, I dream of a world where I can never hurt anyone.

My only solitude.

The only kindness I can have.

Caroline Sophia Hamel

Dunet

I could tell Myllia. Right now.

Any time I could.

But that would be selfish. That would be too horrible, even for me.

Isn't she going through enough?

Do I even care about her? Since when was everything about me?

I thought that I wanted to make everyone happy.

Yet, my words threaten to slice from my lips. To burst out of my chest and find something, anything ... anyone to latch onto ...

That person could only be Myllia right now.

Who else would it be?

Not mom or dad.

It would break them too much.

I already broke Liela.

Of course, not Liela.

Not Torie, she reminds me too much of Liela. Not Kreenie, she wouldn't get it and she's too cheerful. And I don't feel like I know Lunan enough, even if I like him. I don't feel like I know any of them.

Darnor maybe ...

But my skin itches ... that he knows too well ... or that I would somehow cut him too deep.

He's made it clear that I'm family to him, and I love him like family ... but I just don't know how I feel about that.

And Driena ... it sends a shiver up my spine. She looks at me weird. I wish I hadn't noticed. When she stares at me too intently, I want to turn my eyes away and I find myself squirming.

Myllia is the only one I feel safe around to not overreact, and she's trusting enough that I can trust her not to tell ... as horrible as that sounds. I feel comfortable letting myself show my hollowness around her.

I know she's too kind. I know it will be heart-wrenching for her, but she's too soft. I don't deserve her. I just hope I don't break her heart too much.

I decided to talk to her before. So, I know that I can do it again.

My stomach twists oddly, but I find that I don't mind.

Occasionally this newfound emptiness is a kind of bliss.

I was ready to snap.

Or maybe ... I just tell myself that ...

Caroline Sophia Hamel

Those Who Seek Our Souls

Dunet

"Dunet." Her voice pierces me. It cuts, like the time I tried cutting food behind Liela's back and cried when she found me. A feeling when you want to run from what you did and do everything perfectly, even when you know you've actually done nothing wrong.

To me, everything I've done is wrong. I must be perfect for everyone.

I twist my hands behind my back and tug on a broken, sunny smile. "Yes?" From my lips, it sounds like sunshine.

She narrows her eyes, then huffs, relaxing. "I knew this would be hard." She mutters for a moment, then crosses her arms. "You know your relationship with Liela bothers me." She taps her foot fiercely for a moment, her arms crossed tightly over her chest. "So, I want you to tell me straight up, what's wrong?"

I flinch. My head cocks to the side, after my eyes briefly snap wide, but it's a delayed reaction. My heart feels far too alive, and I can't think. "I ... I don't understand." My grip's tight. My weight shifts and I look down. "Everything's fine." My voice comes out small. I knew from the beginning that Driena hated me.

"Dunet." Her voice softens just enough. "Can you look at me?"

I look up slowly, but my eyes linger just below her gaze.

"I know I'm not the best person for this. I was never a people person, but I hate Liela like this. Either you change or she does." Her voice is hard and cold, but then I see her look away at the top of my vision. "I just don't want something to happen like with my sister. You're a good person, just like Liela. You're well-intentioned, just like her … But you're too bright for your own good. I can see it. I know I have trouble too. Frankly, I'm trying. But for Liela's good, this is what I can ask of you. I could care less. I want to like you … I just—people like you bother me, but I see so much of myself in you. You just confuse me, Dunet."

My tongue feels twisted and I try so hard to meet her gaze. She makes me freeze up, but does a part of me like this? Does a part of me want her to see me?

"Just think, Dunet. That's all that I can ask of you. I don't want my best friend broken over you. And I guess … that I don't want you broken either. One thing that I can tell is that you got this twisted kindness from her. You got too much of it for your own good and I hate to say it, because sometimes I think Liela is too perfect. I look up to her. As someone who thinks of her as a sister …"

I finally meet her eyes, my vision wavering and my heart cold. This is what I hated her for. This is what she took away from me. My heart pounds for several seconds and my mouth is dry. But at the same time … this is the most alive I've felt in ages, and I want to go numb from feeling. "I'm scared." It's all I can get out.

She gives me the faintest smile. "You really ought to be." Then she laughs lightly, approaching me, and sinking to her knees. I want to back away, but I keep my legs tense, though my feet shuffle back the slightest fraction.

"I'm not good with things like this, but …" She gives another smile and brings her arms around me. It's not the warmest hug, but my arms come around her shakily. "You and Liela are both so much stronger than you know. I think if you looked past your fear, you could be brave. And I think maybe … I think I could get myself to like you. After all, I'd follow your sister to the ends of the world. I respect her more than anything and I want to respect you." Her voice is just a tad harsh. "I want to stop seeing things that make me want to hate you. I know it's unfair, but I often feel that nothing is. It took me so long to get that and put myself together in the best way I could. I'm satisfied with that. I never wanted to care about you, but I see Liela needs you and you need her." She unwraps her hands abruptly and her smile fades as quickly as it appears. "If you care about her, do this for me. Maybe I'm wrong to say this, but it's what I know, and you deserve my honesty."

I want to say that she would be a better sister to Liela. I want to say that she should take my place. If anything, she deserves it. She cares more. I want to say something to make her happy with me. I want to say anything, but what do I say? What I do say is always the bare minimum to not upset anyone, to keep everyone happy with me, to feebly try to make others happy, to say anything to keep from freezing. But now, it's far less than that, because all I can manage is to nod numbly and give an "Okay."

When her eyes inevitably harden and she turns away, I just whisper. "I'll try." I know that I really don't mean it. I long for something to take my mind off it. Anything. An abyss. Something sharp. Sleep. Cold. A story, if I actually wanted to be near Liela or had the urge to read. Riding. Cooking. But really, I would rather do nothing.

Whatever spark came from her words, it fades away in an instant. Because she knows I'm just pretending for myself, and I don't even know why anymore. It's something I just do.

In a Gentle World

Myllia

Maybe I've been a sobbing mess lately ...

But my chest seems to lighten just a bit. I have Liela by my side and a future in front of me.

No matter how much my heart breaks or how heavy it is ... for I don't think it could ever heal ... I have something worth giving, and that is what matters.

For the first time in days, things are starting to look bright again.

I dab at my eyes, as Liela sits next to me on the white bedsheets. My heart accelerates and I think she sees the look in my eyes, so raw and asking. I have wanted her for so long, needed her, and this time she doesn't turn away. Instead, she folds into me, her arms on either side of me. There's a knowing gleam in her gaze and a rise in her breath when she leans down and kisses me.

I think we're both ready for this.

Our mouths pull together again, softly. My lips tingle each time hers meet mine, and my heart builds to a steady, fast rhythm.

When we pull apart and our eyes meet, my eyes are soft and filled with every meaning I want to get across to her. I know that now is the time that I can ask.

"Liela, I want to share *every* part of me with you."

She looks into my eyes for a moment, and she nods, her dark hair draping her shoulders like a veil about to be lifted. Her voice comes out quietly, but confidently. "I want that too, Myllia." For a moment, she raises one of her hands and places it delicately on my side. There's a pause in that touch, then she lets go with a pensive wrinkle on her forehead.

"Is it all right?" I ask her, my heart still racing. I already feel warm all over, like my body is a step ahead of my mind, but I don't want to pressure her into doing something she is uncomfortable with.

Thankfully, she nods again, this time closing her eyes for a second. "It is, Myllia. It's everything I want now." Her lips break into an eager smile.

My heart ascends so full, skipping all its beats.

I move forward into her, her body soft in my hands.

Her hands move to my waist and I wrap my hands behind her neck, tugging her gently back into a kiss. I close my eyes and can taste the sweetness of her mouth, like fresh berries picked out in the fields. For a moment, I am swept back to our spot beneath the shade of the tree, by the water. The feeling of us together here, now, brings me home to spring, to summertime. Flowers are blooming.

Tenderly, she touches my cheek, and her mouth opens in a delicate laugh. "Myllia."

"Liela." I begin to undress, reaching up to unclasp my bra while my eyes tease her. Once I'm free of the garment, I move to unclasp her bra, but she grabs my wrists, surprise widening her bright eyes.

Before the question leaves my mouth, she goes to help me unclasp it. Then, practically shaking with excitement, she pulls me closer and plants a few big kisses on my cheek.

Giggling, I turn my head and catch her lips. We're both smiling so much that it's now hard to kiss, so we switch to just feeling each other.

Somehow, I wind up above her, looking down at her tall, lithe frame. Her hand brushes gently over my shoulder to push back my hair.

Her eyes seem to observe me. All of me. It makes my heart quiver.

I'm a little nervous, for some reason. But that feeling passes as soon as I feel her hands drift back to my hips. "Myllia ..." she breathes, lifting her head up to kiss my neck. A shiver runs through me and in no time I've removed her underwear.

I lace one of my hands with hers when we lock our legs together, growing nearly frantic with our movements. Staring into her olive eyes and their beautiful, endless depth, it feels as if we've been transported to a world where only the two of us exist.

I roll over on my side, curving into her. Her arms reach behind me and tangle in my hair, as mine reach down to the warmth of her back.

Caroline Sophia Hamel

Our hips sway and rise against each other and I feel the goosebumps of her skin, her heartbeat racing with mine, her bare form the most beautiful thing I have ever seen.

Her skin is as homelike as I could've imagined. She is my home, and my future.

I arc into her touch, and she pushes her hands against my back.

My hand falls between her legs, and she moans passionately, her back curving into the feeling. As I rub her, her hands move up to my breasts, holding onto them.

"Myllia," she gasps, eyes glazed over slightly and an adorable smile on her face, "keep going."

"Okay, Liela." With my free hand, I move her head closer to mine. This time, when we kiss, our mouths open. Something feels different now between her legs, and her whole body tenses up and shudders for a moment. I stop what I'm doing, though I'm unable to look away from her blissful expression.

The pleasant grip on my breasts loosens, and hand presses between them. I move a hand over hers, letting her feel my heartbeat.

"How are you, Liela?" I asked, checking in.

"Great," she breathes out, sincerity shining in her eyes.

We're both panting, our eyes locked, and breath mixing.

I never thought she could be this beautiful. More than she was. It melts my heart.

She rolls over me and kisses me, her gorgeous hair cascading over my collar bones, and I let my body collapse onto the blankets as she lays into me.

The bed quivers under us and she brings her mouth to my breast as I lean my head back. The amazing feeling stops for a moment when she pulls up. I don't want it to end, so I catch the curve of her hips and move against her. Her mouth meets my breasts again and the pleasure builds until I spasm in pleasure, trying my best not to cry out too loud when I grab at my breasts, trying to make this pulsing sensation less intense.

She continues to move against me. As she does so, she bites at her lip, releasing a small sound that sends my heart aflutter. I'm compelled to sit up with her on my lap, kissing her breasts while I touch her lovingly below.

Suddenly, her legs tighten around me and her head dips forward. She moans into my shoulder, shaking just as I had a moment ago.

Both of us fall to our sides, facing each other. I lean my head on her shoulder, my arms wrapped around her. I want her close. I *need* her close. This is the most connected I've felt with anyone, ever. And it makes my heart soar knowing that I will continue to feel this way for the rest of my life.

She wraps hers around me, still panting.

"I love you, Liela," I whisper with my eyes closed. "I never want this moment to end."

"Me neither, Myllia." Her voice sounds like honey, as her fingers comb through my hair. "I love you too."

I open my eyes, casting them from her caring smile to the moon just past the shroud of curtain. I feel grateful for everything.

For the person I love.

I giggle softly, in a daze, and I curl into her chest. The last thing I hear tonight is her heartbeat. It's the most lovely sound, in the gentlest world.

Time That is Ours

Myllia

I wake up with her beside me. We're curled into each other. Her form is beautiful and fragile in the morning light. I smile, and giggle under my breath.

"Myllia." She pulls herself up, stretching her arms above her head, before her eyes go wide at her bare chest and she abruptly drops them, her cheeks red. She laughs to the point of giggling uncontrollably, shaking her head, then holds onto me. "I may be a bit embarrassed, Myllia."

I giggle again, my heart soaring— it's a pleasantness in my chest. "Good morning, Liela." It leaves my lips so gently, as I hold onto her. "I love you." I never thought I would say those words like that.

I know now that I have everything I want and need right here ... as we hold each other close in this silence that is ours ...

Liela

I lay against her for as long as I can. I never want it to end, as I feel her soft heat and all the curves of her plump body nestled warmly against me.

I never want to open my eyes to the daytime. I'm in a dream. A dream I never knew I wanted.

But I have my duties. Unfortunately, I can never get away from them.

"I have to go, Myllia." I pull my eyes open and meet her lips.

"Liela." Her eyes are glassy, but so clear and lovely. "This is the happiest I have ever been."

My heart stutters, and I nod. "It is for me too." I slowly push myself off the bed after one last kiss, wrapping our arms around each other and catching every intimate touch of our bodies, just savoring it. I move to the closet to get dressed, all too aware of Myllia's eyes on me, my cheeks burning.

I'll have to get used to this. And I will, because I want this to last.

I can be anything for Myllia. I can be my full raw self and lay my heart bare in a way I never could before.

That's one thing I love about her.

As I move to the bathroom, my smile as I look in the mirror is more than my own. Twinkling. So much fuller than I've ever seen it.

Despite every reservation I have, my heart bursts in a way it never could've before. And I know this world I am in is a gentle one.

Time That Stops

Liela

I thought that night may not come again. And maybe it did not come the same, but there's something so warm about sharing so much of myself with her. I stopped being afraid of it and, at last, let in all the warmth of us.

I'm too busy and tired much of the time, but some nights are our special ones. And I suppose I'm glad she put into words that she wanted this. I never would have, or at least ... I never thought I could. But sometimes, I want to be with her enough to tell her.

I think she knew that, and she was probably afraid for me. I wanted to be ready for this, as much as it scared me.

She pulls close to me again. My eyes are moist as I unbutton my shirt and she drops her bra. Her lashes flutter at me and make my heart ache.

She brings her lips to mine, and she tilts her head back just as I inch into her. Then she looks down between my legs with a teasing smile and a blush on her cheeks.

What is she thinking?

Lowering herself to the floor, with the heels of her feet resting against the soft fatness of her butt that I can't help but look at, she holds my thighs in her warm hands and moves her face between my legs.

Caroline Sophia Hamel

I squirm, biting my lip when I feel her tongue against me. My legs begin to quiver, but I keep myself from collapsing. A soft moan escapes me and my fingers run through her hair.

I surprise myself when I don't move her head away.

This is almost too good to be real. I attempt to press my lips together when I feel a louder moan of pleasure coming from deep in my chest. I catch an amused glitter in her eyes when she glances up at me, and I can't help but burn with embarrassment.

But it's a good kind of embarrassment; I love the way she's teasing me, bringing me to the edge, making me blush.

She pulls back her tongue and rises to her feet. When she kisses me, my head begins to spin. I can taste us both.

"Myllia," I say her name, although I don't know what I had planned to say.

"Liela," she copies me, giggling.

I know what to do now. It only takes a moment for me to get down on my knees and reciprocate. She's sweet and warm, and she feels so soft on my squeezing hands. Her hands push my head gently toward her as she spreads her legs, and I can feel myself burning with desire.

I look up and see the desire in her eyes—she's beautiful and voluptuous and perfect, her thighs spread between my hands. I move up to feel her abundant hips and the mound of her belly; her large chest rises in exertion, her cheeks red at my touch. Her eyes close in pleasure, something that makes me feel joy and love for her. There's no one more beautiful than her; no one I would rather share myself with. As if nothing else matters.

I laugh a little in my head. I want to be naughty like her, as I let myself go. Let myself be fun, but more than that—let all that rigidity go. That fear that I need it and that maybe I would be rejected without it. That I can't be comfortable with myself. For her, I want to be.

To let go and be free in my own body for once. I've never felt that way—not fully, even after so long striving to be me and feeling a bit more like I'm myself each day. I still feel out of place, but in this intimate world, I feel whole. It's enough to be with her and to let myself experience this part of me without shame.

Placing myself between her wide thighs, I go back to tasting her.

"Liela—"

Her body jolts back and her legs shake, eyes closed at my touch. I draw back up her body and kiss her.

She falls back into me, on top of me, her body lush and full.

My eyes close and I bite my lip, feeling all the tension release and my limbs give out. I breathe heavily, lost for a minute in a blissful haze.

She rests against my chest again, smiling and catching her breath.

Caroline Sophia Hamel

After several moments, I feel her plump lips kiss my cheek. I laugh when she kisses each of my breasts before lying on her back and closing her eyes. There's something silly about it that I can't explain, but even without knowing why, I do the same to her.

Her laugh warms my heart. Yet the words "Good night, Liela," make me a little sad.

"Good night, Myllia," I say, wishing we had more time in the day, more hours to spend together. With Myllia, there's a fresh layer of meaning to my life that rejuvenates me.

Well, we shall see each other tomorrow, and we'll sleep side by side tonight. She isn't gone, we're just asleep. I have to remind myself of that.

The world feels pleasant and right with her. Everything that I'm scared of just fades away.

I wish she could be all that mattered to me.

Liela

"So, how are things going with you and Myllia?" Darnor cracks a low grin, a pleasant openness to his eyes. He leans back over the wall—his normal pose, looking leisurely, but his eyes are bright on me, like he knows the answer.

I flush profusely. "Well …"

"Maybe I should stop there." His face turns soft and kind. "The last thing I want to do is make you uncomfortable. I just thought you looked different."

"No," I say, as I relax, letting out a breath. "It's fine. I think I want to tell you, but it's going better than I thought was possible." I feel the now familiar heat of my cheeks, that uncontrollable urge, and somehow it's okay now. For whatever reason, I used to think I would never know this heat personally, and it comforts me that it exists, and I can let go sometimes. "She … well … last night," I stammer. I breathe in, staring up at the sky, then grin back at Darnor, my eyes raw and alive and free from last night. "Anyway, I really am happy. I never thought I could feel this way." My own eyes turn dreamy for once and my voice quiets. "She's perfect, Darnor."

"I never thought I would hear that from you." He smiles fondly. "I'm happy for you."

I close my eyes, laughing into the air. "Hopefully, you would be." I grin and chuckle. "Why would you not be?"

"No idea!" He laughs. "But Liela, you know, I'm always here for you."

I nod, and then, getting over myself, I hug him. "Thank you. You know it means a lot."

"Of course. I can never help it."

I breathe against him. He was always such a good person and a kind friend who could understand me and he knew what I needed when it really mattered. That's one thing I appreciate about Darnor over Driena. He's so much easier to talk to sometimes. I step back. "I want you to help me tell Driena."

"Easier said than done."

"Come on." I sigh. "I'm a little … scared, though."

He shakes his head. "Liela. We both know that she's kinder than she lets on."

I nod. "I know that, but I told you first for a reason."

"And now I can let her know you told me first!"

I roll my eyes. "I had my reasons! You're not that special, Darnor."

He scoffs, lifting himself off the wall. "As if I didn't already know."

"Well, at least you can both tease me now."

"The pleasure is mine!"

"If I allow it"—I wink, then give a sweeping bow, arms outstretched—"then the floor is all yours!"

"As you command, Commander." He winks.

I break down into a fit of laughter, bracing myself against the wall. My knees buckle.

Darnor's eyes gleam, as he covers his face and joins me. "If we are not the sight!"

"We are!" I catch my breath, closing my eyes to relive the pounding of my heart and every new sensation from last night. It can never leave me, like I'm in a new world. Like I won't wake up, in the best way, from this dream. A beautiful dream that hardly fits into my reality, but at the same time ... does perfectly. I tug on his arm, lacing it through mine. "Come on! Now is a better time than any to doom my future!" My heart really feels erratic. At times, Driena is as easy to read as a sister, but sometimes I don't know what to think or what she thinks.

Darnor and I find our way on the carpeted expanse of red, below the high-ceilinged hallway between the two wings of the library, gray cascading through the skylights and opulent chandeliers hanging from the ceiling, large marble columns to both sides opening to the expansive library with its nooks and crannies and the students studying in candlelight, hearth light, and shadow.

Darnor's footfalls and my own play in a synched rhythm, a testament to our friendship and his intentional-or-not humor of the moment, to try to lift me up.

My footfalls feel light, lifting in a way that's not in my normal stride. A few people look up, eyes curious, and I adjust my footfalls to their usual practiced cadence, removing my arm from Darnor's as he falls into line.

He whispers sidelong at me. "I think they think we're crazy!"

I cover my mouth, turning to him with a glimmer. "Oh, they think we're idiots! But … I don't care as much lately. There are times when I just want to let go …" I sigh a little.

"Careful," he chuckles. "Or maybe they'll wonder where the Commander's gone."

"On vacation," I breeze, whipping my head back slightly.

Darnor's eyes are slightly wide. "I think she is."

"Really, Darnor, I don't think you know how draining this is. Far worse than your studies!"

"One would hope." He turns his eyes about absently, but they still gleam.

I look ahead, grin still plastered to my face. But beyond that, I'm composed once more.

Well, I suppose destiny told me that we would find Driena in our alcove in the library and not in her office or elsewhere, and I was unfortunately very right.

"Liela." She looks up with a smile.

Darnor clears his throat and Driena ignores him.

"Yes." I roll my eyes. "Driena knows that you're there, Darnor."

"At least acknowledge me."

I hold my face straight as Driena fails to make eye contact with him and sits up, lacing her fingers and looking at me. "So, what is it, Liela?"

Darnor scoffs.

"Okay, Darnor. Is that enough?" She looks to him, her eyes suddenly less stern.

His smile is playful. "I think so."

She looks pointedly back at me.

I hesitate for a moment, looking away. Then I look back. She's my star-soul, my sister. How couldn't I trust her? My eyes go blurry at her image. I love her as one, and that should be enough. I know she loves me, and that's enough. That's all I need to let these words out that have built up inside me. I no longer want to keep this a secret from them, no matter what happens. "I wanted to tell you, Driena. Really, I wanted to tell you earlier. But ... I'm in a relationship. Her name"—it comes out in a breath— "it's Myllia."

Her eyes go wide and my heart drops.

I swallow. "For a while ... She was my friend, we met in a courtyard, she was ..." My words start getting mixed up in my dry mouth. "She ..." I grasp for the right words. "I fell in love with her." Every little part of my consciousness latches onto Driena, my heart stuttering and goosebumps forming along my flesh. I want whatever happens to be over.

She shakes her head slowly. "Liela"—she huffs after a moment, arms crossed— "For once, I don't know what to say."

My blood strains on her words, mind frozen.

She smiles lightly. "But I want to support you. I really never thought you were the type. I see it, though." She shrugs. "And I meant in general."

I look at her for a moment before the tension dissipates just a little. I shrug, my mouth still dry. "I suppose I am."

We hold a small look between us for a moment, and then her face breaks and she's laughing raucously, bent over slightly, still shaking her head.

Darnor cracks a grin and I join him, all that tension transforming so cathartically that I'm nearly crying.

"Liela"—Driena pauses—"You don't have to take it that hard." Her smile is pleasant and softer somehow. "I'm with you. You're my sister in every way that matters. Maybe

I don't understand or get it, but I'm with you. If you say you love her, that's what matters to me."

I nod several times, feeling numb, my eyes welling.

She gets up, walks over to me, and pulls me into a hug. "You're never alone."

I shut my eyes, tears pooling and spilling.

"I was always and will always be here for you, as your sister." I swear that I hear her sniffle. She pulls away, wiping her thumb below my eyes with a gentle smile that kindles at my heart. "Because that's what we do for each other. Because you're my star-soul."

She pulls away. My lip still trembles and my body still shakes a little. I nod again, my shoulders still quivering. "Thank you, Driena."

"Liela, it's only for you and Darnor. You let me be me. I want everything for you."

I nod several times, biting my lip and swallowing. "And thank you, Darnor."

He closes the distance and hugs me. "The same for everything. It's always worth it. I always will want to be there ..."

I choke back, opening my eyes. "I love you both."

Driena nods with a smile.

Darnor grips me harder. "I love you, Liela. You're a one-of-a-kind best friend."

Driena meets my eyes, hers turning so deep in the moment. "I love you too, Liela … I always will."

I nod again, as the tears run furiously and Darnor grips me harder.

Sometimes, I'm such a crybaby.

But these tears are light, lifting me to a place I never thought I would be, with two friends who mean the world to me.

I love you both.

Forever.

Who I Hate the Most & The Love We Hate

Dunet

I rest my head against the wall.

I've made it a habit of finding places no one will find me in.

I love them for hiding me, making me feel safe and letting everything collapse on just me.

The sky is gray today.

I don't want to do anything. I can't face anything.

All I have is nothing.

This presence in my mind, these thoughts ... me. It's what I hate the most.

I hate me the most. Only me and no one else.

I always feel cold.

I hate that people say they love me.

It's not me that they love.

I hate that look in their eyes.

Not them ... but I wish they would get away from me. I'm no good. I've done nothing for them.

Every day, I just want to disappear.

Everything is dead in my eyes, but it's really me that's dead ...

Caroline Sophia Hamel

Why is it me who gets adoration? Why is it me who gets love? Why isn't that enough? Why is my smile no good?

And yet, no one can see that I'm drowning. I never want them to.

It's just me—a cold, empty chill around me. There's nothing, only vague sounds and images that I barely latch onto.

I hate that I want help. That I scream for it.

Most of all, I hate that I want love.

I'm too selfish ... to have decided that I'll ask for help and hurt the person that I do.

A part of me wants to. A sadistic, awful part of me wants to do anything that hurts them ...

How would they even feel if I died?

Would they cry, or would it be a mercy ... a relief?

I know, I think about death, and dying, and these thoughts should never seem like a reprieve ...

But they do.

I want to tell Myllia, if only to push her away ... She'll see how ungrateful I am for all her efforts, for Liela's, for Darnor's, for everyone's ... She'll know I really am awful. Selfish. Unworthy of what everyone else seems to have.

That's all I have left to do.

The hardest part will be when it gets time to tell Liela and crush her like I've crushed Myllia.

Because, if I still have them, then I can't do this.

They are … no, Liela really … is the only person I live for. I cannot erase what would happen if all still believed in me, and I were to do what I want desperately to do. If they were still in my life, believing in me, I don't know if I could do it to them … If I could leave.

So, I need them gone. I need them to stop caring.

The Love We Grasp For

Myllia

Dunet called for me.

I pass through the hallways, chiseled and neat, and I feel a chill woosh through them. I can't know what to expect. I put on a smile, hoping for the best. I ascend the winding stairway to the Lord's suite. This walk feels familiar now. It sets my heart at ease and slows my mind.

To me, Liela is my home. Dunet is too. I never really had a family that felt like one.

I find myself in the familiar passageway of their home, warmly lit, soft carpeted, and with the lovely tapestries Liela's mother adores. I always wonder about her—what kind of woman she really is. Why she gave up on Liela. But from Liela's talks about her, she gives off such a composed, graceful air. I know it's not my place, but I want to meet her, if only to bring her and Liela closer.

I reach Dunet's door and knock lightly. I still haven't abandoned any of my own upbringing. My posture, my walk, my light knock on the doorframe—it's still just as ladylike. Sometimes I forget that I'm no longer a lady. I certainly won't be able to afford a carriage much longer. I giggle—but that just means we can walk to town holding hands.

My stomach mixes oddly at Dunet's reaction to us. She seemed so far away. Supportive, of course, but there's a sinking in my heart for her. She wasn't present, and I don't think she wanted me to notice. I know she wants to be there for me, but I think she knows that I can't unsee what she's told me up to this point.

I crinkle the fold of my dress and slow my breathing. I want to be ready. I want to help people. I want to heal people. Dunet is important to me.

It's the mindset I hold close to my heart. It shakes sometimes, but whatever comes, my desires are enough. My wish for my own world is enough. A wish where I can be me and help others express what they cannot to others.

Dunet creaks the door open, peeking at me with a disheartened expression, behind her spryness that looks forced. "Myllia!" She stands on her toes, giving a familiar, but wavering, smilc.

I look her up and down. "Dunet, is everything all right?" She looks just barely put together and haggard, but everything is far too neat. She covers her wrist and I notice a flicker of red. For a moment, I thought they were nail marks. Her eyes look too drawn—like she hadn't been sleeping much. Just enough splotched makeup to cover it. I'd never seen her wear any and it almost looks ridiculous on her—enough to laugh—but I don't, because of the plummeting of my heart and my dry throat.

Her eyes dart across my face and she nods. "You can come in, Myllia. Would you like to sit down?"

I take a position on the bed, below the painted stars and doves. Dunet hesitates, feet inching in my direction, and she clutches her stuffed bunny, Ceilia, tightly to her chest. Then she nearly runs over to me, but everything about her is small, as if she can't bear being too close right now. She seems almost skittish, every line jumpy and hyper-aware. She settles down far enough that my heart throbs at the distance between us.

She looks like she needs a hug, and I want to give her one.

Her eyes turn down. "I suppose I don't look all right." She pauses, trying to draw her breath once, then again, with more confidence behind it, hand steady and eyes solid. But those eyes are dark and my soul aches for her. "I'm a selfish person, Myllia." She shudders, but her hands are tight, in fists. "Sometimes I wonder if it were better if I weren't here ... if I were gone." So much conviction comes into those words that it tears my heart apart. So much effort, and an underlying loathing that makes it hard to breathe and to hear. I wish I hadn't.

She's too young.

I sit there, stunned, everything too silent and Dunet too lonely and too far away. I clutch at some words, even though it still hasn't sunk in. "Do not say that, Dunet. Can you not see how much you mean to Liela?"

Her face goes too hard, too cold for her age and for her. Her words seem to slice the air, from a depth I never knew she could have. Nothing I could've imagined. But I think I figured out that it was there. "I can, but I can also see how much pain I bring her—how worthless I am."

I stare at her, my eyes prickling and my chest tight. Panic crosses my mind. I want to run to her and do … something. I feel overwhelmed, making it hard to know how to get across to her or to process. The realization of the depth of Dunet's pain hits me like a wave in my chest. She can't mean that …

"Dunet"—my voice feels dry—"You are a beautiful, caring person." I put every ounce of effort and softness into these words. "You are sweet and kind … You make others happy. You make Liela happy … Please, Dunet. Do not sell yourself short. You care, and that is a good thing. You care far too much …"

She shakes her head, her eyes distant. "I know what you think, but that's not who I see. I only care about myself …" she trails off bitterly. "I'm a selfish person, Myllia." There's a silent darkness of conviction in her eyes—a silent storm beneath all that sunshine.

"Dunet … you are …" I'm at a loss, my voice reaching. "Do not tell yourself that. You have a spark that made Liela who she is … It made me who I am now. I took these steps because of you … You are not worthless, Dunet, or selfish." I feel desperate to find the right words, knowing everything I could say could be what mends or breaks her.

She starts bringing her hands to her ears, shaking. "Myllia." She squeezes her eyes shut. "Stop. Just stop. Okay?" Her voice sounds empty, tired—too old and too pained.

I know she doesn't want it, but I try to reach for her, knowing she needs it, and she flinches. I draw my hand back, hurt cracking at my heart.

I stay silent, grabbing my dress where I think she won't see. I clutch it like a lifeline, even though I know it will do nothing. How do I get through to her? I want to help her.

What do I say? My hands start shaking and I hide them. My eyes are wet, and I quickly wipe them. I don't know what to do with this horrible sinking feeling ... this fear that someone as young and pure as Dunet could think that. That her thoughts could be so dark and haunted and alone. "Dunet ... I love you. I want you to live. I need you to live." I mean each and every word. I know that in my heart. "What do you need?" I try to be patient, try to listen, even as it's so overwhelming that I can still barely breathe or think it through. This is what I wanted. To help her. I don't want to make this worse for her. I don't want to be what drives her to that. I need her to know that I'm here.

"Don't worry, Myllia." She meets my eyes from that lonely darkness, even if they don't reach me. "I can live with this." Her eyes are broken, though, and I don't believe it. Because she doesn't deserve it, no matter what she thinks about herself. She deserves a happy ending. "I just wanted to tell someone, and I couldn't tell Liela." It's like she's screaming for me in the quiet. "I'm sorry ... for bringing so much on you ... for worrying you. Especially with what you're going through. I'm selfish. I just ... It's weighing on me, and I needed to tell someone ... before I snapped." Her eyes look lifeless, joyless, and I want to turn away from them and their pleading. "Please do not tell Liela. Please, Myllia ..."

I stare at her, my heart lost in a storm. I don't know how stable she really is. I don't want to leave her alone, now that I know how she feels and how deep her hurt is. My fear is so overwhelming and for once, nothing can control my breathing and my racing thoughts, like nightmares that get away from me. I feel heavy, and the only reason I can still function ... is because she's here ... in front of me, with those desperate eyes.

"Myllia." She places her hand over mine. Her eyes are clear and searching. Trusting and layered. "Thank you. I feel better now. I promise not to do anything. Will you promise not to tell Liela?"

I look down tentatively at her hand and all that trust contained in her small palm, ready to break with the wrong words. My stomach roils, and my mind is at an uncertain crossroads. I shake my head in a daze.

"Myllia ..." There's a soft need to that one word. A desperation and an edge of pain.

I shake my head slowly and the small warmth and hope start to fade. "I am sorry, Dunet, but that is something I cannot promise. Not when I know this."

Her face turns withdrawn. Cold.

"But as long as you promise to keep putting your trust in me"—I take a shaky breath, wondering if I'm making the wrong decision—"then I will know I haven't lost you yet." I want to trust her. If I have to compromise to keep the trust between us, is that the right thing? Or am I pushing her to the edge? Is this worse for her?

She looks at me, that timid warmth returning—her wariness receding just enough, and her grip loosens, when I hadn't even realized that it was tight to begin with. "Thank you." She releases an exhale, her shoulders sagging, a weight seeming to leave her.

I let myself get close to her now and she lowers her head.

I turn to her, and she throws her arms around me, as if desperate for anything to anchor her, but in an absent way. Reserved, like she's not feeling it. I hug her tightly—so tightly—to let her know that I'm here—that she means something to me, and that I will not let her go. I love her now and it brings me such pain. I just need to hug her.

She's shaking so much, but it's hardly noticeable. It's stiff and detached, and I know she's scared.

She grasps me back, a little girl again, and I can feel her shaking violently now, her tears starting to fall onto me in a wave of numb, cathartic relief.

I let myself fall apart then too, a mix of relief and dread and confusion and panic, but I hold her close, trying to tie her to this world.

I need her, I realize.

I shudder as it occurs to me ...

Maybe, sometimes, it's the ones who appear the happiest ... who are really hurting the most.

It is a somber thought that makes it hard to breathe. To stand still in this world, when someone like Dunet needs me. How could I never notice all the pain around me?

My heart aches for her.

Caroline Sophia Hamel

The Love Between a Chasm

Myllia

I feel a twisting in my stomach—to trust Dunet or betray her, so that I don't risk losing her …

Liela looks at me, so uncomprehending and hopeful—innocent. How I wish Dunet looked. Her other self.

I can't shake the emptiness I saw in her eyes.

To betray Dunet, or betray Liela?

I feel sick.

Should I trust Dunet—that she's stable enough to live—that she wouldn't lose too much of herself so as to hurt herself and cause Liela pain?

Or would it hurt more to tell Liela, to have her face that truth, when in my heart, I know that Liela would never consciously hurt her sister? It's the truth I want to believe.

I choose Dunet.

It rings so coldly, with the barest of hopes and the barest of warmth.

"She is okay." I cannot find a smile in my voice, knowing the implications of my choice. "She will get better." I want to believe it.

I see a bittersweet smile on her face. "Thank you, Myllia. At least, I can know that much."

A shiver runs down my spine at her words. "I know she will be, Liela. She has you." I give a comforting smile. I hope that it's enough.

"Myllia—" She sighs, putting her hands to her temples and looking at me warmly from under their slender length and the dark browns of her hair. "I know you've been there for her much more than I have. I just want to say, thank you." Her olive eyes are too soft for me right now. It breaks my heart.

And it doesn't feel quite right. How could I ever tell that face?

I look at the resignation there and my chest squeezes. How can I possibly bring them together when they're so far apart? "You have been there, Liela, and you will. I just pushed you two a little closer." But did I even do that? Because they're both more lost and hurt than they ever were.

"I wish every day that I could be there for her more." She stares out the window, over the brushing curtains, to the dusted mountains, her hand clutching at the blankets. "It's ironic ... that in wanting to protect her, I just pushed her further away. No matter what, I really couldn't protect her in the end ..."

I squeeze her other hand. It feels so frail. "You had to let her grow."

"I know. I see that every day. She made me confront all the ways I hadn't grown up." She tugs on a small smile. "Or, at least, I hope so. Sometimes she seems so much older, like she's the one pulling me up, more than I am for her. It should be the other way around." Her voice is a soft, gentle mourning of a girl that feels lost.

"And you see that now." I press on her cheek across the sheets, forcing her to look at me. "You have realized something that not every sister or parent could, Liela." I look affectionately into her olive eyes, becoming lost in how gorgeous they are, and drawing her forehead to mine, so that I can see her clearly. "I chose you, Liela, because you were kind and caring. Passionate and driven to do what you thought was right. You cared and you showed it. You grew into yourself, and you faced your fears, no matter how hard that was. You cannot see everything, Liela, and to me, you handled it brilliantly. You let her know you love her—that you wanted the best for her. Liela ... she is still scared, but I know you will always be there."

"Myllia ..." she breathes it, and it tickles my skin. I want to kiss her. I want everything with her. But all I need is her here now, just to make my heartbeat race like this.

"Liela, I love you."

"I love you too, Myllia. Thank you. I am ... I want you to know that I will always be glad that you wanted to be with me. I think I need you just as much as Dunet needs you right now. I know she can't trust me with everything like she once did, and that maybe she never did. I never gave her the chance. She's lucky to have someone as kind as you."

"She is just as lucky to have you. I will always be there for her, Liela."

"I know you will. You shouldn't have to be."

I squeeze her hand and her other hand comes away from the sheets to wrap around my wrist, tracing my fingers. She still looks embarrassed sometimes, with her eyes timid and her posture stiff. It makes me giggle and she looks away with a blush, before laughing.

"I can never get used to this."

"And that is why I love you. You are adorable when you're awkward." I weave my hand around hers. She's too much for me sometimes—I feel like I'm rushing for so much more. "Good night, Liela."

"Myllia ..." She grips my wrist tighter. "Just before bed."

I scoot over, giving her a soft, slow kiss that sends butterflies through my chest, before pulling back to see her self-conscious smile. I know her well enough to know that was all she was asking for. And for now, that's enough for me.

"Good night, Myllia."

I move closer to her, trying to reassure her more that I'm here. I can see her staring off at the ceiling and I just smile lightly, with the barest twinge of grief. Dunet will be all right, I tell myself. I'm sure of it.

I trust her.

When We Fear Love

Liela

I walk out across the frosted lawn, the morning silent and the sunlight springing off the thin blanket of snow. The Kalltarris Mountains stand silent and beautiful in the morning, snow-covered and never changing behind the familiar castle and weaving of courtyards. The stables are before me, the fields stretching so far out beyond them. It is a morning beautiful like any other, but it feels sad, even as my smile rises in thin hope.

Dunet and Myllia are already out, Eriena and Ina saddled and Vel held in Myllia's hand, ready for me to mount. Myllia smiles at me fondly.

Dunet stays where she is but looks to me with that same hopeful, reaching look she has started to give me, her smile small, but there. It's almost like there's something else underneath it, which I want to shake off—something that looks haunted.

The first flurries start to drift, blanketing the world further. The sun still peeks from the open sky to the east.

I tense up for a moment as Myllia gets down next to Dunet and whispers something in her ear. Dunet nods, looking at me with her head cocked and a faded light to her eyes.

She runs up to me a few moments later. "Sister, it is good to see you." She says it with a broad smile that compliments her red mittens and scarlet headband, with her tan winter boots, crimson scarf, and white, winter dress. Her smile seems brilliant in the moment and her eyes alight like I haven't seen them in a while. Everything about her seems bright—her honey hair, sapphire eyes, and soft, childlike face, fair rosy cheeks filled with energy as she hops. But she looks harder, almost piercing. And did she ever wear headbands before? She loved having her hair a mess ... It feels wrong. Such a tiny detail.

My breath comes out slowly, haltingly, but with a smile. "It's good to see you too." I don't know what to think of her calling me *sister*. It feels like an apology each time—like a reminder of the girl she was. I chastise myself—she's still that girl. Still, it feels odd coming from her now, if also heartwarming at the same time. "Are you ready to go riding?"

She hops again but stays an arm's length away from me. "I am! I saddled Vel already." She looks down. "I am glad you came. I know you're busy and that you don't have time for me. I know that it takes a lot to come to my lessons ... I just wanted to say—" She hesitates, seeming to push something else away. "Thank you."

The distance between us feels impossibly huge, but so close. "Dunet, I do want to be there. Thank you for worrying about me. I just wish I could spend more time with you."

"Liela." She looks at me directly, her sapphire eyes radiantly clear, like they're burning. It makes me shiver. "I will do this. Whatever it takes, I will be ready."

I look into her eyes, full of that new confidence—intense and unwavering. I take her hands, trying not to tear up and to keep my voice level. "I know you will." I kneel in front of her, pulling her into a hug. "And I will be right beside you. Ask me if you have any questions, okay?"

I feel her nod, and her still small grip around my back. It makes my throat constrict.

"You have Father, too … and Mother." I sniffle. "Father will mentor you. It will be some time yet before he passes this to you." I feel like I'm letting her go. What if she really doesn't want this?

"I know." That statement is simple and certain.

I brush her hair, pulling back again with a warm smile. "Would you like to go riding now?"

She nods. I can see the lingering hesitation in her eyes. It's something I would've missed before—would have dismissed and ignored before, or just couldn't have caught. There's a chill to even acknowledge it.

I try one last time and it's an effort to keep my voice steady. "Dunet, is there anything else you wish to tell me?"

She shakes her head slowly. "No … No, Liela."

I falter a little, but let it go.

I get up and Dunet turns away from me, running back towards Myllia and Eriena. She mounts Eriena, looking at me from over her shoulder.

I smile, even if I want to brush the sting from my eyes.

I keep my stride over to them and help Myllia into the saddle, my fingers tingling on contact with her luscious form. She blushes at me and my heart flutters weakly. She turns to look at me purposefully and my chest blooms, before it starts hammering. "Get up with me, Liela." I can see that teasing in her eyes, but that soft consolation next to it that manages to soothe me and make my cheeks hot at the same time. It's always like she's trying to take my mind off my worries.

I laugh merrily, my chest tickling and warm in the moment, eyeing her with touching whimsy and hoping my gratitude also gets across. I move up in front of her and she brings her thick arms around my waist, kissing me softly behind my ear. "Take us out, Liela." I tilt my head, kissing her in return, and she closes her eyes at the kiss, giggling as I pull away.

We start moving out and I can hear Eriena start into a trot behind us, gradually moving to catch up.

I can feel every beat of Myllia's heart and her lush body against mine. My own heart cartwheels to feel her this close. I'm happy to spend every moment I can with her.

Myllia shifts in the saddle to cast her gaze back at Dunet. I glance back to see Myllia sending a worried look at her. I wonder at that, and my skin crawls. Why don't I understand Dunet as well as she can? As much as I'd like to push down that shred of jealousy, I can't.

I stiffen a little without realizing it and I can feel Myllia's arms tighten around my waist. I loosen up a bit at the reminder that she's still there and that she's there for me. She leans into me, resting her head steadily against my back. I breathe out, "Thank you, Myllia." She just squeezes me again.

I know I am grateful to Myllia.

I am content to know that she is who Dunet needs right now …

~ End of Book 2 ~

Caroline Sophia Hamel

There was a girl who chased dreams

Until she found her own

She was a timid girl

An absent girl

Who lived in a fantasy

And chased it to reality

Made it her own

And found

That she was much more than she ever thought

And that girl

Is much stronger

Than she ever let herself dream

The world is hers

And it calls for her

To bring it her gifts

To weave the world from her dreams

For her dreams were worth living

Once they were found

She found her voice

Caroline Sophia Hamel

Acknowledgements

First, I want to thank my beta reader, Paige Downey (paigedown on Fiverr), who read the first complete draft. You've been a lot of help to me, and you're very timely and professional. When you looked at this, I was still uncertain and insecure about much of it, and I thank you for your patience and understanding. Because of you, I have a lot more faith in this book and it's always a pleasure working with you.

Luke Shealy, thank you for the early feedback on what would extend into this book. Thank you to you and to Katherine Atkins for pushing for more of everything. This book was never meant to be a series. I scrapped the ending for a better story and honestly, these books and their message is better for it. And I will always thank Elena Irish for being my original reader. If you end up reading this, I hope you love it as much as the first. You've always been my biggest inspiration to keep writing.

Thank you again to Rachel Johnson for originally giving me this opportunity and thank you to Chloe Hovind, Chelanne Evans, and Jessica Moreland at Village Books for all your help. You've all been a major help in my publishing journey. And my recent transition to retaining full control over my own publishing went so much smoother because of you. Thank you for your patience. While I am now publishing on my own, I will forever be grateful for the immense amount of time the four of you have put in that made everything so much easier and less confusing.

More than anyone, I've loved working with my editor, I.O. Scheffer (Ellie). I continue to trust you more than anyone with my books. You always know the exact right things to make my books better and you have such an amazing understanding of my characters. I can't begin to say how much I trust you and I continue to love working and talking with you as a friend, as business partners, and as fellow authors. I am immensely grateful to you for some of your rewrites, including helping me to heavily revise / partially rewrite my sex scenes. Your rewrites brought me so much joy. I laughed and subsequently cried from reading them. No one else could have done them. You perfectly captured my characters, while beautifully expressing everything I wanted and was trying to express in a way I just couldn't. And there's plenty of other things I'm grateful for, and so many things I could just bring up with you and that I got so much out of when talking to you. You're an amazing editor and I'd highly recommend you. You're also an amazing author. I'll say it again and again, but I love your books so much. For anyone reading this, I'd really recommend reading I.O. Scheffer's Fearghus Academy series. It's a magic series with so much heart. And it has an amazing autistic lead that is really relatable. I.O. Scheffer is another LGBTQ and neurodivergent author, who 100% deserves more love and support.

Thank you so much to Chii (@mihaellustrates) for the gorgeous new cover. <3 I've wanted Myllia on the front cover for a while. Chii always illustrates her so beautifully and I honestly don't think anyone else could capture her or do her justice as perfectly as she does. <3 Myllia definitely deserves to shine on her own cover. She's still my favorite character I've ever written. I also really love more art of Dunet and Eriena together, so I adore the bittersweet back cover too. I'm incredibly happy with the covers and as always, grateful for more of Chii's gorgeous art. And I'm happy to have such a sweet, kind person as my friend. You can find plenty more of her art on her accounts (@mihaellustrates).

While I've retired my old cover art, I still want to give a thank you to my original cover artist, Sophia Lindstrom (@sophia.lindstrom.art). I'm still very fond of the old covers and you can find them on my website. They were delicately beautiful and I'll always be grateful for the work she put in.

I want to thank my sensitivity readers: Katherine Holst (@kh_reads), Mary Warren (@fatgirlsinfiction), Sandra Blasco (@readswithsandra), and Marie Tucker (@fatandfabulousbooks). I appreciate your input in improving my rep in this book (and in the revised edition of To Hold a Flower). It's important to me that Myllia's depiction is relatable, sensitive, accurate, and tasteful for all my fat readers. I'm continuously learning how to portray Myllia more authentically and in a way you love and I appreciate your help. Your feedback was invaluable and you've provided me with so much helpful information that I can reference. You've given me even more ways that I can beautifully depict and express Myllia and I'm so happy for it. Thank you to all four of you for providing your thoughts. I look forward to working with you in the future.

I also want to thank those of you who participated in my cover reveal: Sandra Blasco, Marie Tucker, I.O. Scheffer, John North, Tina Capricorn, and Caroline Marie Wolff.

Thank you to the composer, Yuki Kajiura for composing music that's immensely personal and enjoyable to me. Her music helped me through a lot and it's special to me. She's been my favorite composer for nearly the past decade of my life. I love everything she's involved with, whether her scores for various anime or songs for FictionJunction and Kalafina. And thank you to orchestral music in general for inspiration, comfort, emotion, and enjoyment.

I specifically associate the composition, "Cradle" (the piece from *Pandora Hearts*; she's composed two pieces by the same name) with this book. I also named a chapter after a different Yuki Kajiura piece, "in a gentle world." While the context of the original piece is different, it captures a similar bittersweet feeling of finding moments of love and comfort amid pain. For a song, I think AURORA's "Winter Bird" fits Dunet a lot.

I'm grateful more than anything that I met my best friend, Martina through this book. <3 It means a lot to me how much you fell in love with Myllia. <3 Thanks for being such an amazing friend. <3 You're the most amazing, wonderful, kind, and beautiful person in existence. You've come to mean a lot to me and I'm forever grateful you came into my life. I love you and you deserve the world. <3 Also, I hope one day you're a world-renowned author, because your stories are incredibly emotional and well-written.

Author's Note

In a way, this book was more isolating than the first. Everyone's pain was emphasized and on display, their dreams, their joys. This book feels even deeper and more personal than the first. Darker and more intimate. When characters were in low points, struggling to move forward. I think that in a lot of ways, The Essence of Longing is an even more raw exploration of my characters. They reach their lowest and highest points yet. And sometimes that's ugly. By design, they are less likeable, in a way. They reflect what we hate most about ourselves in a lot of instances. Our darkest thoughts that will either make you understand them or hate them. Dunet especially, being my self-hate, goes to a very dark place. And I hope that, however hard it is, some of you needed a character like that. And maybe she is empty now, but as I slowly piece her back together and heal her into a full person, who loves and appreciates herself, I hope you can heal too. Because Dunet, like I had at one point, is gradually going to a place that no one deserves.

For Dunet, this book is about isolation and struggling to keep others happy as she is drowning in her own thoughts. For Liela, it is keeping her world together, while she feels tossed around in a world she cannot control and is losing grasp of, wondering if she is doing the right thing. For Myllia, this book is about her taking control of her own life and finding who she is. She realizes that she is more then who she is with Liela. For me at least, this book is Myllia's. It is her book to shine. Maybe it is not a straightforward path or an easy one, but she chooses to take it and trust in herself.

I will admit that this book was initially going to overwhelmingly feature Dunet, and it was going to be a much darker and more painful book, but then I started getting really invested in Myllia. This book is truly about Myllia. She's the star of this book and I want to acknowledge that. More than anyone, she represents hope, as she moves forward with confidence into her future.

Myllia's arc is about her growing into herself and her confidence. It's exciting, and more than a bit bittersweet and emotional. Myllia's growth and confidence, pursuit of a career she loves and cares about, her job searching, and her fears of coming out, are all reminiscent to a degree to some of my own experiences. Maybe she doesn't tie in as closely to me in ways Liela and Dunet do, but she still is a character I place my experiences in. And I forever wish I could feel free to express myself with the confidence she can.

In a lot of ways, I am guessing this book was hard to get through, though I hope that there was also plenty of hope, joy, and self-discovery that it shown through more than the depression. There were less highs, even though they were still there, and more depressing lows. Honestly, thank you. These characters deserve the world and so do you. Maybe everything feels dark right now and maybe it will never be perfect, but one day it will be better. There will be a day when you start to heal. Maybe this was a dark entry, but to me, this is an optimistic series and I like to think the messaging and character arcs are overall optimistic in this book. I promise a hopeful, bright ending. I thank you for coming through this book with me.

The next two books, I plan to lighten it up a bit, before going really intimately dark, before the healing starts for Dunet specifically. I know I keep highlighting Dunet, but to me, I write for people like her. Yes, for people like Liela and Myllia too. But suicide is close to my heart. People drown and break and feel alone, and I want to be there for them. For you.

I want you to find yourself. Maybe you are suffocating now, but you deserve to feel alive and to feel loved, to feel whole, and to move forward as yourself.

There is still so much left I have planned in my character's arcs, and I hope you will continue reading. Because this book is for you, as much as it is for me.

An In-Depth Discussion of The Essence of Longing's Themes

~

Suicide, Depression, & Self-Love

This is why I write. I write so that people can learn to love themselves.

I've struggled with suicidal ideation and depression for several years. Suicide is a topic near to my heart. I've known several friends who attempted to take their life and I nearly have as well.

I felt empty for the longest time. I felt like I had nothing. No one deserves this.

Healing is hard and loving yourself is hard. It takes time. The least I can do is to tell you that you're not alone, but I'd like to do more. By the end of this series, my characters will love themselves.

I almost committed suicide twice. The first time is closely paralleled in the last scene in To Hold a Flower. I felt I had nothing left and overreacted in a situation involving my mom. I misread her, we miscommunicated, and I thought that she didn't love me anymore. She's the most important person in my life. The two times where I was ready to attempt suicide, were the two times I thought I lost her love.

In my content, I frequently deal with characters in my stories working towards self-love, self-worth, self-acceptance, and confidence in themselves and their strengths, as well as finding meaning in life. Many of my characters feel selfish or empty. But I also balance my work with levity, because there is so much brightness in this world.

I hope that by sharing my struggle with suicidal ideation and healing, it will help some of you as well. You deserve to be here.

Caroline Sophia Hamel

Loneliness & Isolation

Dunet's loneliness and social isolation largely stems from my personal experiences not feeling understood, the exhaustion of masking and trying to navigate a neurotypical world, and a combination of being burnt out and guilty from feeling like I'm always doing something wrong. Most of her depression comes from guilt and extreme self-hate from trying to make everyone pleased with her to blend in but it not being good enough, so she feels like she's still letting people down and is undeserving from feeling like she's constantly acting as a people-pleaser.

Her social isolation is both in social situations and in the more literal sense of removing herself from everybody. In social situations, she has no idea what's going on. She's often confused and can't figure out how to connect with others. And the more she feels that way, the more her depression grows and she physically isolates herself.

Her loneliness stems from the same reasoning. She doesn't know how to connect with people, and she doesn't understand people. And people don't understand her either. She always feels alone and separate from people, like there's a wall dividing them. She really wants to be understood and have friends and she misses having connections she hardly understands and barely knows. It makes her sad and feeling more than a bit empty in the world.

The physical isolation this leads to (which is sometimes self-harm, in how she doesn't care about her health) is realistic to me.

I don't know where she'll end up with relationships. For me, I've found happiness and contentment being alone. Not completely, as I still have anxiety and some depressive episodes, and I can live with myself now. Friends are often too exhausting and stressful for me. But I don't really know what ending I want for Dunet. Personally, I'm planning on never giving her a romantic interest, but I probably will have her form some healthier attachments with trust, understanding, and freedom. Again, to what degree I'm unsure. I know that in some ways, she'll always be a bit of a loner.

Caroline Sophia Hamel

Consent, Boundaries, Communication, Establishing Healthy Relationships, & Sex

Part of my goal for this series is creating and depicting healthy relationships.

This includes consent, boundaries, and establishing communication. Consent is arguably one of the biggest takeaways from this installment in the series, and something I've worked up to gradually. Consent is to receive someone's agreement and comfort before (and during) any sort of physical contact. My goal is to normalize asking for your needs and asking for the other person's comfort. I handled this heavily on the topic of sex in relationships and to a lesser degree with kissing and physical contact. I believe consent should apply to all forms of physically intimate contact, including—and perhaps this is controversial—asking for consent before a kiss, which is something I'm working towards depicting more.

To be honest, depicting sex was something I was hesitant to do. My mindset around sex has honestly been pretty conservative and abstinence-oriented up until recently (I've never had sex myself or been in a relationship, and at this point, I no longer want to be). It was a topic that I wasn't planning to handle until Liela and Myllia were married (okay, yes, they're getting married, but I think you can expect that plot point from me by now; after all, my books are hopeful, and I will give queer people what we deserve, but so often don't get). But my ideas and understandings have changed and I no longer hold that view.

I felt very strongly about depicting sex in a healthy way. I hope I did. Healthy sex is based in mutual consent and communication. Sometimes people aren't ready or aren't communicating well, and I wanted to show that. While I didn't always lean into this message as much as I could have, I believe Liela and Myllia's relationship is a mostly healthy one.

I also do want to point out here that this relationship could have very easily been a much less healthy one, given Liela's disability and Myllia's vulnerable emotional state after dealing with her parents. If Myllia weren't such a good and well-intentioned person, there are several instances in these books that could've easily led to Liela being taken advantage of (like when Liela had a shutdown or didn't understand what's going on, which I do suppose Myllia acted / imposed herself upon Liela's vulnerability several times, and I do think that's not the healthiest on Myllia's part, even if it did end up working out for the better), coerced (which is why I wanted to have a clear conversation about consent, because Liela would have gone along with whatever Myllia wanted, regardless of what she herself actually wanted), or manipulated (though, I suppose Myllia still did lie to her, even if it was to protect her). Up until partway through this book, it's mostly been Myllia guiding the relationship, and Liela letting her do it, while being less aware of her own desires and the nature of her relationships. Liela starts to become aware of her feelings, and she gains more agency in the relationship. At the same time, Myllia exercises more agency in her life outside Liela. They're sort of working for what the other person has, in a way, and it was fun to explore different sides of both of them as they opened up and experimented with who they were and what they wanted.

My relationships are all strengthened by better communication—this is necessary to understand each other and be in the same place in a relationship.

I don't mean for my relationships to be all-consuming. My character's have lives and dreams outside their partners. And my characters still need personal space. Boundaries are a way of balancing a relationship with a sense of self. Sometimes it's okay to take time away from your partner, and it should be encouraged. Boundaries can be used to deescalate situations and lower stress. I also wanted my characters to not function as solely a love interest. Myllia isn't just a love interest, but her own person. This is why she has such a clear arc of self-determination. This relationship was a choice, but it isn't all-consuming. It isn't her entire world. I want to depict relationships with freedom and with personal choice. In other words: relationships without control and without overemphasis on a romantic partner.

Myllia's Agency

As stated above, I wanted my characters to have agency outside of their love interest. In the first book, Myllia's agency was mostly tied to Liela. This was something that I found relatable, but I wanted to do something more with her.

Over the course of this entire book, Myllia is claiming her agency and deciding what type of person she wants to be. This is an important step in her journey that I think a lot of people can relate to. It's cathartic and exciting. And being the person she is, she wants to do what she knows that only she can do.

She's finding her voice in this book, something that she's expressed in her conversations with Liela and with Dunet. It's always been there, but she's never truly used it. In this book she finds empowerment and a purpose, and I hope her arc motivates you to embrace your strengths and use them for good. She's unapologetically claiming who she is, and I think that's powerful, inspiring, and something to look up to. Her dream is worth pursuing.

And while she pursues it, she never loses what makes her Myllia. She's still feminine and expressive and unapologetic. She doesn't have to lose her femininity to be confident in the world, and she doesn't have to feel shame for her fatness or queerness. Myllia is someone who embraces who she is, no matter what the world throws at her, because everything that makes her, her, deserves to be seen.

Myllia's been my more impulsive side. She's my side that's confident, but unlike Liela and Dunet, she doesn't care what other people think of that, and she won't let others hold her back. When she wants something, she does it, sometimes without thinking. I wanted to show that that could be used as a strength and for good. Because Myllia has a lot of good in her.

I think Myllia's empowerment has a lot that's exciting to it, and in my mind, it provides a balance to Liela, and especially Dunet's struggles in this book. Even if she does struggle herself, she never lets that hold her down.

A Note on Fatphobia

Lastly, someone's weight does not equal health or a moral failing. Everyone has a different healthy body weight and you can't know what it is just from looking at a person. It's none of your business whether you think a person is healthy or not and I'd encourage you to keep your fatphobia to yourself and maybe rethink where it comes from. Fat people deserve to live and thrive without stigma, invasive comments about their bodies, diet, and lifestyle, and medical discrimination, just like everyone else.

Codependent Relationships

This has probably become very apparent, but I've largely been codependent on other people. This results in me putting my entire self into other people. As a result, most of the relationships in this book have leaned into various degrees of unhealthy codependence. I often hyper fixate on a single person to my own detriment.

While I don't believe that codependence is necessarily bad, to an extent, I'm trying to find a healthy balance between being reliant on others and being dependent. I'm honestly still figuring out how to go about showing this balance. My views on codependence have changed recently, as I've figured out I'm neurodivergent. Because I am disabled, it's often helpful and sometimes necessary to have help from another person in many settings.

Most of these codependent relationships are tied to a lack of self-worth, and near-obsessions with others. Again, I think there's a healthy balance in codependence, but I don't want my characters' entire worlds to be taken up by another person.

LGBTQ+ Themes: Sexual Orientation & Acceptance

Myllia being disowned was a large and potentially triggering part of this book. I understand that may be hard, and my heart goes out to any queer person who's been disowned for being who they are.

I've never been disowned myself. There are times when I feared I would be, but I'm fortunate not to have been. It still took a long time for me to be fully accepted for who I was, and those experiences did hurt a lot. I put my fear and confusion into Myllia being disowned, but I also showed her standing up for herself and being unapologetically herself. Maybe not all of it, but I hope I handled it well for anyone who has been disowned. I hope you found hope through what she went through. What's important is that she found people who loved her. She had people who supported her for who she is. I know found family is important to a lot of people. Myllia found a family in this book. I think that's beautiful. I hope that each of you can find people who truly care about and love you for you and not who they think you are.

In this book, both Liela and Myllia experiment with their sexual orientation. Myllia has been sure of her sexuality for a while, but this is the first time she's expressed herself so intimately and been so true to her heart. And Liela didn't realize she was a lesbian for the longest time. In a lot of ways, she's only just realizing what it means to express and feel comfortable in her queerness. This is the book where she starts taking agency over her identity. Myllia's already accepted her identity, but Liela's still in the process of moving through it.

Liela's Mini Arc: Letting Go of Shame / Unmasking Neurodivergence

Liela has a more subtle unmasking arc in this book. She had a short monologue directly reflecting on this theme. This did happen through her romance with Myllia, particularly in the sex scenes, and in a friendship scene with Darnor. Her revelation, unrestricted joy, and letting go of her insecurities and shame didn't have to be through sex (letting go of your insecurities is an internal change), but I chose to have this growth for Liela tie into the sex scenes due to how taboo I've always viewed sex and sexuality and because of my insecurities around sexuality and sexual topics. I find these feelings of letting go of shame all the more cathartic for that reason.

Liela is a very stiff and restricted person. To fit in, she holds herself to very rigid standards and blocks off a lot of her unscripted, genuine behaviors and personality. It isn't conscious, but she's deeply afraid to be herself. She only got this far by suppressing the things that made her unique. Throughout both books, there have been occasions where she's let go and expressed herself around those she trusts or acted in the moment, but this is the first time where she hasn't cared or reverted her behavior to avoid judgement. She doesn't care if she's silly, embarrassing, or unpalatable. Her trust in Myllia overrides all the ways she tried to blend in, and for once is her full self.

This is furthered in her prancing through the library with Darnor, where she's silly and genuine in public, something she's been so afraid of being rejected for.

A Note on Neurodivergence

Liela masks really strongly. She's stiff, rigid, and practiced in her words and actions for the most part. While she's learned how to become a respected commander, it comes at the expense of Liela not being able to naturally express herself and let go. She rarely lets herself go, and when she does, she's really dramatic and spontaneous in a way that sometimes catches people off guard. My neurodivergent characters also have unconventional and seemingly random humor from making seemingly unrelated connections other people don't. Liela is often oblivious and doesn't pick up on things or is slow to take in information. At a few times, she freezes and has difficulty processing words or situations (like mini shutdowns; more apparent in To Hold a Flower). She also gets frequent intense breakdowns / meltdowns to stressful situations, overwhelming emotions, or too much sensory information (the latter shown more in the next book). She has trouble thinking and often has a disproportional response to a situation (something shared to an extent with Dunet). This will be something that becomes a lot more apparent when the siege takes place. She's hyperfixated on her sister to the detriment of everything else, and she almost always finds a way to bring any conversation back to Dunet. She's often all Liela can think of. Most of the time, Liela is hyperfocused and has intense tunnel vision. She has trouble multitasking her thoughts. For the most part (up until recently), her career has played into her strengths, enough that she can mask, be hyperfocused, and be respected. She's very awkward too. She comments on being well-liked, but she really doesn't know how to have a close relationship outside of her small circle of friends. Her being in a field she's passionate about helps her blend in. Liela is also very intense in a lot of her interactions. I honestly didn't realize this until someone pointed it out.

Dunet can't follow conversations and often guesses at responses. She instinctively laughs and smiles at things, even when she's unsure whether she should. Her responses are often short scripts, that are simple and delayed. She is a personification of much of my shame and guilt. I mask by being an intense people pleaser and a strict rule follower, even if I very often don't understand what's going on, and Dunet reflects that. She also has heavy abandonment issues, which neurodivergent people often display, because we have difficulty maintaining long-term relationships. Both Dunet and Liela rely on other people to help them through social situations (it's more subtle with Liela, but Liela relies especially on Driena and later Myllia). Dunet has auditory processing difficulties, which are common in autistic people. It takes her several seconds to process information, so her understanding and responses can be delayed. This makes it especially difficult to follow and understand group conversations, as it feels like a bunch of unintelligible and often distressing noise. Dunet has trouble with eye contact (not necessarily a neurodivergent trait, but for an autistic person, it's hard to multitask looking at someone while simultaneously processing what they're saying). And the more Dunet masks, the more intense she gets (something Liela comments on at the end of To Hold a Flower). The points Dunet is projecting the most confidence, she often is forcing eye contact and scripted speech. As the series goes on, she gets increasingly blunt, in ways that are sometimes unintentionally rude, hurtful, or not socially appropriate. She gets more shutdowns and sometimes has unrealistic flight responses. When she's experiencing sensory overload (more sensory information than she can process), is emotional, or confused, she'll go into a shutdown (or a meltdown, though less often than Liela). She has difficulty with facial expressions and tone and sometimes appears blank and monotone. And she shuts down when things get overwhelming. I will say that some of her joy was real, while some of it wasn't. Her joy at the beginning of To Hold a Flower was undoubtably real. She often appears much younger than she is. While some of her joy is an act, some of it is her semi-freely expressing herself. She's also drawn to animals, because she feels they can understand her better. And her stuffed bunny, Ceilia is her comfort object.

Kreenie is often tone-deaf. She's incredibly energetic, spontaneous, and childlike. She stims (child-like movements that help with emotional and sensory regulation, like her hand flapping) and has an eager, unaware way of explaining herself, talking about things, and expressing herself. She appears rude at times she doesn't mean to be and is unaware of a lot of the negative tension directed at her, or the tone of the room in general. She's loud, bubbly, and often out-of-place. She often doesn't notice or stick to social rules because they don't make sense to her, and like many of my other characters, has a spontaneous, whimsical humor. And she does several things that would make other people embarrassed without realizing that she should be embarrassed. She's honest and blurts her thoughts. I do plan on giving her a special interest in the next book that she'll talk a lot about and probably show off. A special interest is something that a neurodivergent person has difficulty not thinking about and puts most of their attention, thoughts, and often conversation into (if they aren't masking), which can come off as obsessive. She's also very unintentionally forgetful and sometimes has difficulty sticking on one task or line of conversation, which I'll explore later, even though she can be very good at certain things.

Driena is very intense, similar to Liela and Dunet in some ways. She has a "you either love me or you hate me" mindset, she can take things very personally, and she holds Liela, her special person to extreme standards, putting her on a pedestal (which you'll see more of in the next book). She rewrites her personality due to her perceived past failings, feelings of inadequacy, and unresolved trauma, makes snap judgements about people, and her views of people can switch on a dime (explored more later), which can lead to difficulties maintaining friendships. She has a tendency to have a harsh exterior and internalizes a lot of the choices of the people close to her as reflective on her. At times, she comes off as toxic and controlling, which, if her friends didn't understand her and that she does have a lot of well-intentioned kindness, could lead to a much rocky friendship.

Rep List (Confirmed / Shown Rep Only):

Liela – Autism (strongly masking), Lesbian, Anxiety

Dunet – Autism, Depression, Anxiety

Myllia – Fat, Lesbian, Depression

Kreenie – Co-occurring Autism & ADHD, Mid-Size

Driena – BPD (Borderline Personality Disorder), Depression

Ella – Potential Learning / Mental Disability

Helin – Lesbian

Alice – Bi (Bisexual)

Note: Please take everything I say about neurodivergence with a grain of salt and do your own research. I considered cutting the explanations out upon revising the files for the new cover, but for now I've elected to keep those sections in.

Caroline Sophia Hamel

About the Author

Hello! My name is Caroline Sophia Hamel (she/her)! I'm a trans woman, bi / pan, likely neurodivergent, and 22 years old at the time of publishing. It's my dream to be able to connect with, help people, and express emotion through my writing.

I love emotional media, especially beautiful, bittersweet stories that I can deeply connect with. Hopeful stories have grown to mean a lot to me. As someone who's struggled with my identity and mental health, I understand that hope is what many of us need. Even if my own stories may be depressing at times, in the end, I want to show the beauty in the hope in the depths of one's heart.

I've found a place where I've found love and acceptance in myself, even if life can still be hard, I've found myself and a purpose through my writing. I hope that I can help some of you heal. I hope that many of you are able to find connection, empathy, and healing through my characters, especially those of you who are queer, neurodivergent or struggle with your mental health.

Caroline Sophia Hamel

If I can help anyone with my writing, then it's worth it.

I write for a hopeful future. And I want to show you that there is hope and things worth living for within ourselves, even amid our struggles.

Love to you all,

Caroline Sophia Hamel (she/her)

-

If you would like, consider leaving a review for The Essence of Longing on Goodreads, The StoryGraph, and / or another book site. I'm an indie author, so any and all reviews are appreciated and greatly help my reach. Thank you for reading. <3

More Books by Caroline Sophia Hamel

The Illusion We Craved (Book 3 of To Hold a Flower)

Planned for November 2027 (this may change)

The moment Liela dreads has finally come. Claralis is caught in a siege, forcing Liela to use all her strength to defend the people she loves. With Driena by her side, Liela fights a battle to maintain who she is as her anger and confusion only grow. As Driena puts further pressure on Liela to live up to her lofty expectation, that tension slowly begins to open a painful rift in their friendship ...

While Liela struggles with her identity and her friendship, the consequences drive her further into her bitter conflict with her mother.

As Liela fights all her demons and struggles to maintain her mask, Myllia is more committed than ever to doing something valuable with her life. And while Dunet still struggles with her depression, she starts letting people back in just a little, maybe even making friends. She wonders if just maybe, she can be okay ...

To Hold a Flower (Book 1)

A Maroon Star & A Silver Thread

Sweet Girls & Bluebirds (being rewritten)

Caroline Sophia Hamel

www.ingramcontent.com/pod-product-compliance
Lightning Source LLC
Chambersburg PA
CBHW070619300726
48975CB00006B/1861